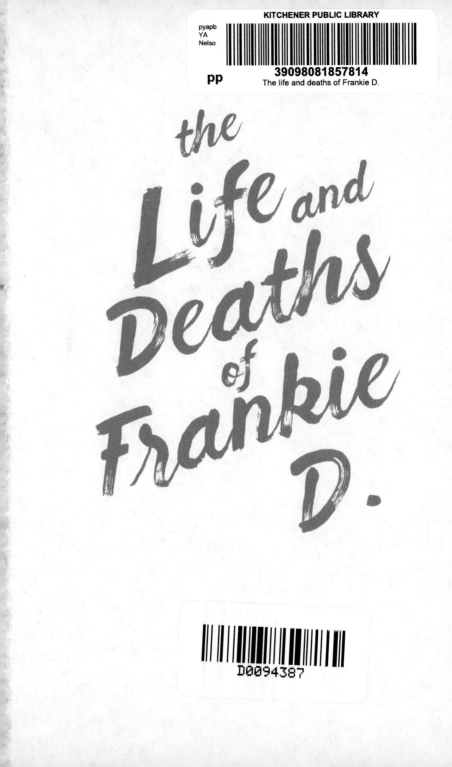

the
Life and
Deaths
of
Frankie
D.

ALSO BY COLLEEN NELSON

Spin
Sadia
Blood Brothers
Finding Hope

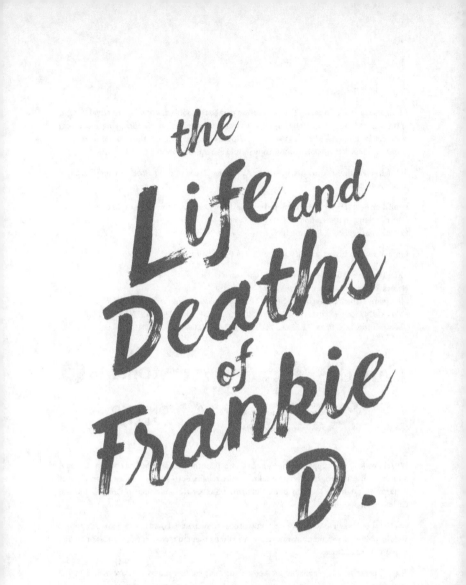

the
Life and
Deaths
of
Frankie
D.

Colleen Nelson

DUNDURN
PRESS

Copyright © Colleen Nelson, 2021

All rights reserved. No part of this publication may be reproduced, stored in a retrieval system, or transmitted in any form or by any means, electronic, mechanical, photocopying, recording, or otherwise (except for brief passages for purpose of review) without the prior permission of Dundurn Press. Permission to photocopy should be requested from Access Copyright.

All characters in this work are fictitious. Any resemblance to real persons, living or dead, is purely coincidental.

Publisher: Scott Fraser | Acquiring editor: Kathryn Lane | Editor: Jess Shulman
Cover design and illustration: Sophie Paas-Lang
Printer: Marquis Book Printing Inc.

Library and Archives Canada Cataloguing in Publication

Title: The life and deaths of Frankie D. / Colleen Nelson.
Names: Nelson, Colleen, author.
Identifiers: Canadiana (print) 20200293249 | Canadiana (ebook) 20200293257 | ISBN 9781459747586 (softcover) | ISBN 9781459747593 (PDF) | ISBN 9781459747609 (EPUB)
Classification: LCC PS8627.E555 L54 2021 | DDC jC813/.6—dc23

We acknowledge the support of the Canada Council for the Arts and the Ontario Arts Council for our publishing program. We also acknowledge the financial support of the Government of Ontario, through the Ontario Book Publishing Tax Credit and Ontario Creates, and the Government of Canada.

Care has been taken to trace the ownership of copyright material used in this book. The author and the publisher welcome any information enabling them to rectify any references or credits in subsequent editions.

The publisher is not responsible for websites or their content unless they are owned by the publisher.

Printed and bound in Canada.

Dundurn Press
1382 Queen Street East
Toronto, Ontario, Canada M4L 1C9
dundurn.com, @dundurnpress

For Isabella

1

THE DREAMS STARTED the night of the break-in. Two weeks ago, my foster mom, Kris, and I had come home from a movie to find the front door open. Every room had been sifted through. My drawers had been dumped and the bed tossed. Kris's, too. Nothing was missing, but Kris was rattled. Break-ins were unusual in our quiet neighbourhood.

It took me a while to fall asleep that night. When I finally did, I had the dream for the first time. Since then, I'd had the same one almost every night.

In my dream, I carried a candle as I walked across a wooden floor. "Hello?" I whispered into the darkness. "Hello? Are you there?" There was no answer. Heavy velvet curtains hung behind me. The planks creaked under my shoes. I was on a stage. A quick burst of air came from behind me. The flame died and I was pitched into darkness. I could hear someone breathing. I wasn't alone. "Who's there?"

I turned at the sound of a match being lit.

A man's face greeted me. He was handsome and wore a top hat and tails, like a circus ringmaster. But he looked worried. "Has he found you?" he asked.

"Who?" I wanted to know.

Before he could answer, the match went out.

That was it. That was the dream.

I'd had it again last night and now I was hunched over my sketchbook trying to get it down on paper. "What's the deal with recurring dreams?" I asked Kris. She stood beside the coffee maker, waiting for it to finish brewing. Her normally flat blond hair was frizzy with some serious bed-head.

She yawned. "Why? Have you had any?"

I nodded and shaded in the man's top hat. "I keep dreaming about the same guy."

Kris arched an eyebrow, intrigued.

"Ew. That's not what I meant."

"Is it a nightmare?"

I shook my head. It wasn't scary … more unsettling. He was worried about me, and I didn't know why.

I finished the sketch and angled my sketchbook toward Kris. She had no artistic talent herself, and she marvelled at what I could create before she'd even had her first cup of coffee. The drawing wasn't perfect, but the concern was evident on the ringmaster's face. "I can't figure out if I'm supposed to be scared of him or not. Is he there to hurt me, or help me? He always asks if someone's found me yet."

Kris didn't say anything, but I'd been in enough therapy to know what she was thinking. "Trust issues, right?" I guessed.

She smiled as she poured two cups of coffee, one for me and one for her. "Could be. It might be your subconscious working through things. You've manifested a person to represent your feelings."

That was a lot of psychobabble first thing in the morning. I stared at the picture, running my pencil along the contours of his face. "It doesn't feel like a dream. It feels real," I said absently.

Kris gave me a long look. "You've been through hell a few times, Frankie. This might be stuff coming up that you need to deal with. Your mind's way of saying it's ready."

Talking about my past wasn't my thing. Nothing good ever came from it; it just stirred up a lot of bad I'd rather not touch. I stuffed the sketchbook into my bag, ending the conversation.

"Your dermatologist called yesterday."

"What did he want?

"There's a support group he wants you to go to —"

I shut her down before she could say anything else. "I'm not going to sit around with a bunch of people to talk about my skin."

"That's not what it is."

I snorted. "That's *exactly* what it is."

I got uncomfortable talking about my skin with Kris. How could I discuss it with strangers? The clinical name for what I had was lamellar ichthyosis, a rare genetic disorder that gave me skin so scaly, it looked reptilian. I shed, too — layers of my skin peeling off like a snake's. I kept it hidden under thick foundation. People assumed the makeup was part of my goth look. It went with the black lipstick, long skirts, studded leather cuffs, and the heavy black eyeliner that ringed my eyes.

"What happened to doctor-patient confidentiality, anyway? Dr. Singh should keep his frigging mouth shut."

Jamming the rest of my stuff into my bag, I pushed the chair under the table.

"Telling me about a support group has nothing to do with doctor-patient confidentiality," Kris said.

There were moments like this when I knew that two years ago, I'd have been raging, kicking over chairs, screaming, punching holes in doors. Instead, I glared at Kris and took a deep breath, just like she'd taught me. *Use your words.* "I don't like feeling pressured to do something that scares me." I exhaled. "I'm not going."

Kris didn't look happy, but she didn't push it. "Suit yourself."

I finished packing up my bag and slung it over my shoulder.

"Want a ride?" she asked.

I raised an eyebrow at her ratty bathrobe and bed-head. She looked like an extra from a zombie apocalypse movie. I shook my head. "No, thanks."

"I'd put on clothes first," she called after me, laughing. "*And* brush my hair." If she said anything else, it was lost as I yelled goodbye and shut the door.

The street was quiet when I left Kris's house. I still thought of it as *her* house, even though I'd been living with her for almost two years. She'd done everything she could to make sure I knew it was my place, too, trusting me with a key, giving me privacy, and stocking the shelves with food I liked. But years of being shuttled between foster homes had left me with a sense of impermanence. At least, that was what Kris said. I was worried about getting too attached to a place in case it was taken away from me. Sometimes I liked that Kris could use her psychologist training with me. But other times, I didn't want things explained; it made them more real.

Mrs. Jenkins, the neighbour two doors down, drove past. I caught her staring at me in the rear-view mirror. She probably thought I was eyeing up neighbourhood pets for some ritual sacrifice. I used to give her the finger, but after fielding one too many ranting phone calls, Kris had begged me to stop. "She's the one staring at me!" I'd fired back.

"She's seventy-two and your outfit terrifies her," Kris had replied. "Of course she stares."

I hated to admit it, but Kris had a point.

Mrs. Jenkins had it all wrong, anyway. Being goth has nothing to do with Wicca or pagan worship. Wearing black clothes was about embracing the dark side of things. Other people saw beauty in sunshine and blue skies. I preferred a full moon at night. To me, *that* was beautiful.

I kept my eyes straight ahead as I walked to school. My armour was on. As usual, heavy foundation hid my skin, and on top of that I had outlined my eyes in thick eyeliner. I'd been experimenting with false eyelashes. When I blinked, it felt like butterfly wings were flapping over my eyes. My lips were stained a deep, dark burgundy. I had been dying my hair for so long, I'd forgotten what colour it really was. I liked the purple I'd been using lately. Chopped into a bob, it hung straight and sleek, covering as much of my face as possible. I had on my leather jacket with studded sleeves, a pawn shop find that I wore all year, no matter what the weather was like, and black gloves with the fingertips cut off. These were more about hiding my hands than being goth.

Henderson High School loomed in front of me. Red brick, limestone stairs, flagpole in the front — it was a totally normal school. There were the usual groups of kids, but I was the only goth.

A group of girls sat on a bench at the front doors. I walked past them, ignoring their stares. The thing about being goth is that it's like an invisible barrier. A silent people-repellant. I shout *Stay away!* without saying anything at all.

In other ways it's like a magnet. Insults like *freak* and *weirdo* fly at me all day long. Even though no one says it out loud, I know they're thinking it. If they call me that when I'm wearing makeup, what would they say if they saw me without it?

I *DON'T DO FRIENDS.* That's what April Beardy had told me when I was eleven years old and asked if she wanted to hang out. April lived in the house next door to Foster Mom #1. Foster Mom #1 was all about normal. But she'd gotten me instead.

When April said she didn't "do friends," she meant she didn't do friends like me. She was the first person to call me a freak to my face. At least the first one I remembered.

It was almost a relief to hear her say it. I could see it on her face, anyway. She didn't try to hide her revulsion. She wanted to hurt me because I was different, which showed that she was as messed up as I was. She was the type of person who'd kick an injured animal or pluck the wings off a butterfly to watch it writhe in pain.

I learned quickly to avoid her and her other "April" friends. They were all like her. Hated me on sight. The months at Foster Mom #1's were brutal. No one knew what to do with me, especially not my foster mom. I heard her having long conversations on the phone with my social worker trying to figure me out.

Eventually, she gave up and it was onto Foster Mom #2's.

The biggest part of the problem was that when I'd been found, all I knew was that my name was Frances. Other than that, my memory was a blank. I didn't know my last name or how old I was. Kris said my skin condition should have made things easier; there should have been hospital records for me somewhere.

But the cops couldn't find anything, which meant either that the records had been erased, which was nearly impossible, or I'd never been to a doctor, which was more possible but completely weird. No one who'd given birth to a baby with lamellar ichthyosis would have wanted to take that child home until they were sure it wasn't alien spawn. Newborns with the condition looked like they'd just hatched out of a cocoon, with a slick sheath covering their skin and their eyelids flipped up. I'd spent hours pouring over photos and medical journals online. I'd made myself an expert in the disorder and probably knew as much as Dr. Singh.

Lamellar ichthyosis was an autosomal recessive disorder, so that meant both my parents, whoever they were, carried the gene. They might even have had skin like mine. But I'd never know for sure, because after gifting me their screwed-up chromosomes, they'd disappeared. I'd been found in an alley by some cops. Even after a months-long crusade by the police and the media to find my family, no one came forward. Were they dead? Or had I been abandoned?

Not having a memory of them was a blessing in a way. It was like stepping out of a dark hallway. There was no point in looking back, because nothing was there. I couldn't miss them, because to me, they'd never existed. All I knew was what came next.

That was what I was thinking about as I spun the dial on my combination lock in the hallway of Henderson High.

I grabbed the graphic novel we were reading in English class, *Persepolis*, which was very cool, and I silently thanked my English teacher, Mrs. O'Brian, for being one of the few decent human beings in this whole establishment. I still had my sketchbook with me, which I'd need for later. The only part of the day I looked forward to — besides the end of it — was art class.

My art teacher, Mr. Kurtis, was the other decent human being at Henderson. He knew about things that mattered. Like, if I mentioned Comicon, he'd know what I was talking about. He'd probably *gone* to Comicon. He knew the band names I drew on my binder, and if I wore a T-shirt with The Cure on it, he'd flash me a knowing smile. The goth thing didn't faze him. Unlike most teachers, he was open-minded about counterculture stuff. He had tattoos on one arm and stretchers in both ears. His hair was always gelled in a swoop and shaved on the sides, and he wore thick black-framed glasses. He was an actual artist — he showed us the stuff he did. Big graffiti murals that he got paid to paint on downtown buildings.

It was Kris who'd figured out art would be a good fit for me. She'd seen me doodling one day when I was in Grade 9 and marched me into the vice-principal's office to show her. I'd barely been going to school back then, so the deal was that the VP would get me into the already-full art class if I promised to attend two other classes.

After my first class with Mr. Kurtis, I'd realized that Kris was right. Art was good for me, like a trap door for the demons to escape. It made coming to school bearable.

Mr. Kurtis let me hang out in the art room at lunch and before school started. He did his thing, tidying up and getting ready for the day, and I did my thing, which was drawing. "Morning," he said when I knocked on the door.

"Mind if I work in here?" I asked.

"Go ahead." He was moving canvases from one side of the room to the other. The room always looked like a tornado had blown through. I sat down at a tall table, pulled out a stool, and took my sketchbook out of my bag. I flipped to the picture of the guy from my dream. One thing Mr. Kurtis was always trying to get us to do was to draw from other perspectives. I kept seeing this man, this ringmaster with his top hat and tails, but what did he see when he looked at me?

Without thinking too much, I sketched the stage just the way I saw it in my dream, with the velvet curtain as a backdrop. A spotlight shone down, and I was in the centre of it. And yet, as I drew, it wasn't me as a seventeen-year-old that appeared, but a child in a white dress.

That was what felt off about the dream. It wasn't me, Frankie — it was a little kid looking up at the ringmaster. Her clothing wasn't typical, either. I drew her wearing a dress with a drop waist. The boots were old-fashioned, with buttons up the sides. When I dreamed, I never paid attention to what she was wearing, but seeing the scene sketched out, I realized the outfit matched the olden days feel of the ringmaster's top hat and tails.

The sound of the morning bell startled me. I hadn't realized how much time had passed while I'd been sketching.

"Hey, not bad for a morning's work," Mr. Kurtis said as he glanced at my sketch. "You did all that just now?" As usual, there were dark smudges on the knuckle of my pinkie finger. I had a perma-callous on my index finger from holding the pencil.

"Yeah."

"Who is she?" he asked, leaning over my shoulder. "Just someone from your imagination?" I edged away from him. I didn't like people getting that close.

"Sort of." I slapped the sketchbook closed. If he'd looked closer, he'd have seen the rough alligator skin that covered her face. Had that been part of the dream? Or was I putting myself into the body of the child?

I took a deep breath before I stepped into the hallway. Hundreds of Aprils rushed past. I'd only gotten two steps away from the art room when a kid rammed into me. He had his hood up and his earbuds in, so I wasn't surprised that he hadn't seen me. My sketchbook fell to the ground, and I stumbled back into a locker. "Ow," some girl said as I bumped her. When she turned to look at me, she bit back whatever else she'd been going to say.

The boy bent down and picked up my book. I crouched beside him. "Watch where you're going," I said and grabbed my book out of his hands.

"Sorry," he mumbled. "It's my first day." His hands shook a little, and I felt a twinge of mercy for the kid. I remembered how it felt to be new and lost.

I started to walk away when I heard him say, "Can you tell me where this class is?" He caught up to me and shoved a crumpled piece of paper in front of me. Dirt was caked under his fingernails. "Bio. Room 301."

"You're in Grade Eleven?" I asked.

He pushed his glasses higher on his nose. The freckles that covered his face made him look like a twelve-year-old. He pulled off his hood. His hair was buzzed and bleached. A few piercings ran up one of his earlobes.

"Yeah I know. I look young," he muttered.

I didn't bother answering. Who was I to comment on looks? "That's my first class, too. It's this way."

Mr. Yeng already had the SMART Board turned on, which meant we'd be spending the whole class taking notes. I hoped the new kid wasn't looking forward to a riveting first period. I sat down in my seat at the back.

"You mind?" he gestured to the empty chair beside me.

"May as well. No one else is going to take it." At Henderson High, I was almost always guaranteed a desk to myself.

"I'm Max, by the way." He leaned in close, and I tilted away from him.

"Frankie." I put on my surliest expression in case he was trying to be friends.

"I like your ..." He pointed toward my eyes, swirling his fingers in their general direction. I raised an eyebrow. "How you drew them."

I snorted and shook my head. He was like a lost puppy trying to find an owner. "Do you have paper? A phone? You need to take notes."

Max looked at me, helpless. "I forgot my stuff at home."

I ripped a sheet of paper out of my binder and passed it to him. "Here. Need a pen, too?"

At least he had the decency to look sheepish when he took it from me.

By the time Mr. Yeng realized he had a new student, class was almost over. "You're not on the attendance

list," he said to Max. "Are you sure you're in Grade
Eleven bio?"

Max grinned at him and held out the schedule from
the office that listed all his classes. "Right here. Period
One." Mr. Yeng took a quick glance just as the bell
rang.

"Aw, the freak has a new friend," said someone behind me. Mr. Yeng hadn't heard and I shouldn't have
turned around, but I did. An April smirked at me. Beside
her was a girl from my art class. She hung out with the
Aprils, but wasn't nasty like most of them. We had art
together, and she smiled at me once in a while.

"What did you call her?" Max asked.

I gave him a sharp look.

"Freak. Look at her." She shot Max a look of disdain,
her glossy lips curling.

"It's just April," I told Max with equal scorn. I wasn't
a fighter. I mean, I could be if I had to. It wasn't that the
words didn't hurt — they did. I'd just learned that no
matter what happened, the girls who looked like me got
the blame. What principal would believe it was the perky
brunette who'd started a cat fight in the bio lab? The good
thing about my armour was that words bounced off me,
most of the time. "I don't care what she thinks," I said.
Other kids were starting to turn and look.

But Max wasn't letting it go. "She's not a freak!" He
puffed up his chest and took what he probably thought
was a heroic stance between me and April. Freckles and
snub nose against cackles and talons. *Good luck, Max.* He
was going to get his ass kicked on his first day.

"Come on," I said through gritted teeth. I yanked
on his arm and spun him into the hallway to follow me.
"She's not worth it."

"Why'd you let her talk to you like that?"

"Like what? I didn't hear anything." Nothing I hadn't heard a million times before.

Max frowned, but I ignored that, too, and picked up my pace. Who was he to judge how I handled the Aprils of the world? Unlike me, he looked perfectly normal, by birth and by choice. Bodies swirled around me, locker doors slammed, kids laughed, feet pounded, and I race-walked to the art room, stepping into the blissful quiet of Mr. Kurtis's sunlit space.

And guess who was still beside me? I gave him an exasperated look.

"Art. Second period." He showed me his schedule.

Mr. Kurtis turned from the sink at the back of the room, where he was washing brushes. "Hey, I'm Mr. Kurtis." He said to Max. "Grab a seat anywhere."

So, of course, the kid pulled up a stool beside me. "Guess you don't have any art supplies," I muttered.

He shook his head. I ripped out a piece of thick white sketch paper from my book and passed it to him. "There are extra pencils over there." I pointed across the room to the tin cans filled with sharpened 2Bs. As he walked across the room to get one, I realized there was something familiar about him. At first, I couldn't put my finger on it, but as I took in his scruffy clothes, the guarded way he watched the other kids, though he'd at-tached himself to me, I figured out what it was. He was a foster kid. Maybe we'd been temporary care together, and that was why he was sticking so close.

I flipped open my sketchbook to the picture of the guy in the top hat I'd drawn that morning. Why did I keep dreaming about him? Was Kris right about it being a weird subconscious thing? Or had I met him before, maybe in one of the foster homes as a kid? Or was he a doctor who'd treated me?

Or was he from my past — the past that was a gaping black hole?

I was about to turn to a new page when I felt Max staring again. But he wasn't staring at me; he was looking at the sketch, his eyes wide with shock.

"You know him."

"Who?" Tingles spread up my spine.

Max pointed a stubby finger at my drawing. "Him."

My mouth went dry. My voice came out in a whisper. "I have dreams about him."

Max pulled his eyes away from the drawing and looked up at me. "Me, too."

3

As soon as Mr. Kurtis dismissed the class, I dragged Max to a quiet spot below the stairs and rounded on him. "What do you mean, you dream about him?"

His eyes darted around, and he clamped his mouth shut. I took a deep breath. This was going to require a little more finesse. I pulled him down to the floor beside me. "Listen, for the last couple of weeks, I've had the same dream almost every night. I'm on a stage. It's dark. Then someone strikes a match, and I see that guy's face. He asks, 'Has he found you?'"

Max tilted his head at me. "What does that mean?"

"I don't know. But it's the same dream every time." I knew I sounded intense, dumping all of this on a kid I'd just met. "What about you?"

"He's in my dreams, too, but he's different. I'm following him. We're trying to find someone."

"Kris thinks it has something to do with my past. Sometimes recurring dreams are a subconscious way of working through things. Trauma and stuff." I hesitated. I never usually spoke this much to someone I didn't know. I wouldn't have blamed him if he'd clammed up and not wanted to tell me anything else. "Maybe he's real. Maybe we both know him. Have you ever been in care? Like with Child and Family Services?"

The shadow that crossed Max's face gave me my answer. His eyes went to the floor, and I knew even before he did that he was going to lie. "I have family," he said. His eyes darted toward the doors. I should have known better than to pry. Questions about family made me uncomfortable, too.

"You live with your real parents?" I frowned as he nodded. *Liar.* But I'd done that, too. Invented the life I wished I had to keep questions at bay.

"What about you? Is Kris your ..." He let the question hang there.

"Foster mom. She's a good one," I reassured him. "And trust me, I know the difference. So, the guy in your dream, does he have a name?"

He blinked at me, and for a second, there was a flash of electricity behind his eyes. "Monsieur Duval," he whispered.

As soon as he said it, I knew that was the name of the man in my dream, too.

"Is it possible for two people to dream about the same person?"

Max shook his head. "I don't know." He pulled his knees up to his chin and picked at a dirty fingernail. The jut of his chin, the slope of his nose, and his freckles all felt familiar.

"Have we met before?"

The bell rang. Break was over. The other kids hanging

out under the stairs sighed and picked up their bags, trudging back to class.

He didn't answer right away, scuffing the heels of his sneakers on the floor. "You tell me, Frances."

The back of my neck prickled at my full name. No one called me Frances. I was always Frankie, which could have been short for lots of things, or it could have been my full name. "What did you call me?"

Instead of answering, he stood up. "I've got to go," he said. Before I could stop him, he sprinted down the hall and out the front doors.

4

"FRANKIE?" Mr. Kurtis stared down at me. "You okay?" The bell had gone for next period, but I hadn't moved.

I took a breath. "Yeah. Just thinking about something." Between my long skirt, my clunky black boots, and Max's weird behaviour, I wobbled a little getting to my feet.

"You sure you're okay?"

"Yeah. Hey, uh, that kid, the new one who came to class with me. Do you know anything about him?"

Mr. Kurtis frowned at me. "New kid?"

If he told me there wasn't a new kid, I was going to pass out. What if Kris was right and all the crap I'd gone through as a kid had come back to haunt me? Maybe I was having a psychotic break or something. Panic rose in me as I waited for Mr. Kurtis to respond. "He sat beside me in class," I said, to jog his memory.

"Oh, yeah. What about him?"

I gave a relieved exhalation. "He looked familiar. Do you know what school he used to go to?"

Mr. Kurtis shook his head. "I didn't even know I was getting a new student."

Except for a few stragglers, the hallway was empty.

"You'd better get to class." He wrote something on a piece of paper and handed it to me with a grin. "Say it's my fault you're late."

I looked for Max for the rest of the week. Scoured the cafeteria, the halls, the library, the stoner hangout doors — anywhere I thought he might go. Every kid wearing a hoodie got a second glance, but I never found him.

If he was a foster kid, it was possible he'd been placed with a new family. Sometimes there was no warning. The social worker just showed up, and as soon as you were packed up, you left. Maybe that was what had happened to Max.

But his disappearance had left me with questions. How had he known my real name? And why did we both dream about the same person? Max had said the man's name was Monsieur Duval, but how did he know that? The whole thing irked me.

All week, the dream kept coming, but small things changed each night. Sometimes I woke up with an extra detail still clear in my head. I got in the habit of leaving my sketchbook on my nightstand. With the image fresh in my mind, I'd reach for my sketchbook and draw whatever I'd seen in my dream. This morning, Monsieur Duval, as I'd come to think of him, had held his arms up in the air, as if to draw the audience's attention. He'd had an Egyptian ankh tattooed on his wrist. It seemed like a strange choice for a man like him.

I caught myself. I was thinking about him as if he were real, filling in his personality where there was none. I didn't know anything about him. Why would I know what kind of tattoo he would get?

"It's just a dream," I mumbled to myself. "It's not real."

Saturdays were chore days, and today, just like every Saturday, Kris had left a list of jobs for me on the kitchen counter while she was out grocery shopping. The usual bathroom scrubbing and kitchen sweeping were at the top. Wash the bed linens and clean the windows. Vacuum. Luckily, Kris's two-bedroom house was small. Our deal was that Kris did the outside work, and I handled the inside stuff. Foster Mom #2 had been big on cleaning. She'd trained me well. I could tuck hospital corners into a bedsheet like nobody's business.

The last item on the list was to clean out the fridge. Ugh. I never knew what I'd find lurking in there. Disintegrating kale from three weeks ago. A soggy cucumber. Guacamole with enough furry mold to make a coat. I'd argued that if Kris did the shopping, she should do the fridge cleanup, but she said that since it was an inside job, I had to do the honours. Plus, it was her house, so she always had veto power. I opened the fridge door and saw an envelope taped to a shelf. It was marked with Kris's handwriting: *open me*.

Inside was a printout of two admission tickets to Comicon. I gave a squeal of delight.

I texted Kris, *Found them!* followed by a string of excited-face emojis.

She replied with a giggling emoji. "Be home in thirty min. Fridge better be cleaned out. I went crazy at the deli."

Comicon, where the freaks of the world united! Nothing was weird at that convention. Actually, not being weird *was* weird at Comicon. People came dressed as anything from *Star Wars* aliens to *Game of Thrones* characters to Marvel Comics superheroes. My skin condition and goth outfits were nothing compared to the blue body paint or full-body tattoos some people wore. It was a celebration of all things bizarre, which made me feel totally normal.

I heard Kris come in just as I was starting to get ready. "I'm back," she called.

"I'm getting changed," I shouted back, staring at my clothing options. Comicon demanded a special outfit. I pulled out my Siouxsie and the Banshees vintage concert T-shirt. I'd artfully sliced the middle so it hung like cobwebs over my leather tights. I added a leather choker and some necklaces. Then, I started on my makeup.

First, always, came the foundation. I'd already applied it after waking up to save Kris from seeing my skin. Now I dabbed on an extra layer, inspecting the chalky whiteness.

The secret to doing the eyes was having a thin-tipped brush and good quality makeup. I ordered mine online. No drugstore-cosmetics-aisle stuff for me. I dipped the brush in water and swirled it in a pot of black eyeshadow. I painted on long black tears bleeding from my eyes. They dripped down my cheek. I used a dark burgundy shadow on my top lid and finished with blood-red lipstick. The whole look was dark and creepy, and I loved it.

I piled bracelets on both wrists, some of them hand-made with safety pins. They stacked halfway up my arm.

My studded jacket sat on my shoulders like chain mail. It was more punk than Victorian goth, but I loved it. It made me feel tough. I'd gotten it second-hand; whoever had previously owned it had worn it in perfectly for me.

I knocked on Kris's bedroom door. "I'm ready," I said. It opened and I burst out laughing.

"Ta-dah!" she cried. Not Kris, but Wonder Woman, complete with the dark wig and red gloves, stood grinning at me. "What do you think? Will I fit in?"

"Totally."

Kris gave me a devilish smile, tilting one leg to show off her footwear. "I even have red boots." They were cheap vinyl, and I doubted they'd survive the walk to the bus stop.

On her way out the door, she paused for a moment to look in the mirror. "I look ridiculous," she laughed, tucking a stray blond hair back under the wig. The thing was, she didn't. No more ridiculous than any other person at Comicon would look. And, standing beside her, I didn't even feel like I was the one who stood out.

When the bus pulled up to our stop, thirty pairs of eyes stared at us through the windows. I realized as I walked down the aisle behind Kris that the passengers were staring at her as much as at me. She met every glance with a smile and sometimes even a "Hello," completely at ease in her costume. She was "normalizing" it for them. That was a word she'd taught me about. Fear of the different made people react with hostility. Kris's friendly behaviour showed them there was nothing to fear. She was just a grown woman in a Wonder Woman costume.

Kris's theory was that normalizing behaviour broke down barriers. What she forgot was that I needed my barriers; they were what kept me safe. We found two empty seats, and I sat down first. Wonder Woman took the aisle seat.

As the bus lurched closer to the Convention Centre, the sidewalks filled with people in costume. Like Halloween for grown-ups. A figure darted in and out of the crowd of people surging toward the entrance. Grey hoodie. I leaned closer to the window. Was it Max? The bus slowed to a stop and I jumped up, pushing my way to the front. "Frankie?" Kris called after me, but I ignored her.

As soon as I got onto the sidewalk, I ran for the entrance. If it was Max, I wanted to catch him before he got inside.

"What is it?" Kris asked when she caught up to me. The wind billowed out her cape behind her.

I scanned the sidewalk. "A kid from school. I thought I saw him." Iron Man, Poison Ivy, and the cast of Scooby-Doo walked past me. Two girls dressed like anime characters with stuffed animal backpacks came next, and then a little person in a perfectly tailored suit.

Kris shivered. She hadn't worn a coat, and the mid-November air was cold. I led the way inside, keeping my eyes peeled for Max. This didn't seem like his scene, but what did I know? I'd only known the kid for two hours and ten minutes.

I kept an eye out for him as we walked from booth to booth looking at T-shirts, comic books, art, and jewellery. There were other goths, too. Whenever we crossed paths with one, I gave them a once-over. Were they just mall goths? Or real embrace-the-dark-side goths? I liked to think my vintage T-shirt proclaimed my authenticity, as did the attention to detail in my eye makeup and hair. Lots of kids thought wearing all black and saying they were goth actually made them goth. It wasn't quite that easy. Kids like that were probably just rebelling against their parents, which made them rebels, not goths.

For real goths, it was just who we were. Not all of us thought of our clothes as armour, but real goths saw beauty in decay and darkness. To most people, a blossoming tree was beautiful. But to me, it was the rotting log on the ground beneath it that was intriguing; all the creatures that scurried in and out, the velvety moss covering the bark, the shadows and crevices created as it decomposed. *That* was beauty. The morbid Victorians had had it right. Why celebrate light and life when death hung over us constantly? Ultimately, that was what we all had in common, anyway.

While Kris talked to a guy at a vintage records booth, I scanned the room looking for Max, or anyone in a grey hoodie. Farther down the aisle, a man walked away from me. He was wearing a top hat and tails, just like Monsieur Duval did in my dreams.

I got chills. "You okay?" Kris asked, looking at me.

"Yeah. That guy —" I broke off. It sounded crazy. "Never mind. I'm gonna look around a bit."

As though an invisible tether connected us, I followed the top hat through the crowd. I got as far as the Batmobile before I hesitated, common sense taking hold. He was from a dream. He wasn't real. I'd only caught was a glimpse of his costume; he could have been anybody. But as the sea of people closed in on me, I knew that if I lost him, I'd never find him again. I glanced back at Kris. She was still talking to the guy at the booth. I stood on my tiptoes — hard to do in my chunky platform shoes — and spied the top hat. Pushing my way through the crowd, I stayed a safe distance behind and followed the man as he wove his way past the rows of tables toward a quieter corner. Once I figured out where he was going, I'd go back and get Kris. If it was Monsieur Duval, I wanted her beside me.

"Frankie?" A kid wearing a hoodie appeared at my side.

I turned in surprise. "Max!" So, it had been him I'd seen from the bus. "What are you doing here?" I asked, then narrowed my eyes. "Nice disappearing act at school."

"I uh, remembered I had to do something."

"Really?" I arched an eyebrow at his weak excuse.

He shook his head. "No. I just don't like school," he said with a laugh. "All the kids and people telling me what to do." He wrinkled his nose. "It feels like a jail."

"It gets easier the more you go," I told him. Kris had said the same thing to me more than once.

Max craned his neck and frowned, trying to see over the crowd. "You're going to think this is crazy —" he started.

"Monsieur Duval? I saw him, too."

Max's expression shifted from confused to relieved. "So I didn't imagine it."

"I didn't see which way he went, though." A guy dressed as Chewbacca walked right in front of me, blocking my view of the aisle.

"I did," Max said. "He went in there." He nodded with his chin at a booth tucked into a corner. Curtains separated it from the rest of the floor. Stanchions were set up outside, and there was a fake ticket booth, like the kind they used to have at theatres. A banner above the entrance read *Circus of Marvels and Wonders* in old-fashioned script.

"Do you think we should go inside? See if we can find him?"

"First, tell me how you knew my name. My *real* name."

He gave me a blank stare. I was worried he'd run again, so I grabbed his arm. He looked slight, but I could feel sinewy muscles tense under my grip. He tried to twist away from me, but I didn't let go, and I met his angry glare with one of my own. With my studded leather jacket and dripping eyes, I hoped I looked intimidating.

"What are you talking about?" he asked.

"At school, you called me Frances."

He shook his head. "No, I didn't."

"You did." But even as I insisted, I felt my resolve weakening. It was loud in the hallway between classes. Maybe I hadn't heard him right. Anyway, why would he lie about getting my name right? I dropped his arm. "Never mind," I said.

Something behind me caught his attention. I turned to look. At first, I thought it was two people, but when they moved through the curtain, I realized it was one person with two heads: conjoined twins.

I peered after them. The same little person I'd seen earlier, when Kris and I had first walked in, greeted the conjoined twins at the entrance. When he saw me watching, he came over.

"Will you be joining us? The show is starting soon." He pointed to a sign in the ticket booth window: *Next show 2:00 p.m.* He came up only to my hip, but his voice boomed.

"Uh, what kind of a show is it?" The booth was so tucked away that no one else from the main floor had ventured over. I hadn't noticed the sign before, either.

"We are the Circus of Marvels and Wonders. Back in the day, before people cared about such things, we would have been called a freak show." He twirled his moustache.

That explained the old-timey writing. It was also eerily reminiscent of my dream and the little girl's dress. Maybe Monsieur Duval was part of the show. And if he was, maybe the recurring dream was some weird premonition. "So, what are the acts?"

The man raised an eyebrow and gave a teasing grin. "You'll have to enter if you want to find out."

I hesitated and looked at Max. "He's in there," Max whispered. "I'm sure of it."

There was only one way to find out. "We need two tickets. How much?" I dug my wallet out of my bag.

"Ten dollars." The man held out his palm. His stubby fingers curled around the bills.

"Come on," I said, dragging Max toward the curtains. "Hey, how long is the show?" I called out to the little man. I wanted to text Kris to tell her where I was. But the spot where the man had been standing was empty; he'd already wandered off.

5

THERE WERE SOME BENCHES SET UP IN FRONT of a
stage. It was a small space with room for only a few
spectators. At the back of the stage was an elaborately painted backdrop meant to look like a fancy parlour. *Trompe
l'oeil*: we'd learned about it in art class. It meant *trick of the
eye*. Max and I were the only ones in the audience. After
we sat down, the curtains at the entrance swished closed.

The overhead lights dimmed and then went out completely. A string of small bulbs lit up along the back wall.
A few candles flickered to life along the edges of the stage,
giving the space a magical, shadowy look. Soft carnival
music played in the background. A heady mix of sandal-
wood incense and something sweeter, coconut oil maybe,
filled the air. The sound of the crowds of noisy people
outside disappeared. I'd never have guessed I was still
at Comicon; the atmosphere of the small stage was so
complete, it transfixed me.

"It's perfect," Max breathed beside me.

On the left side of the stage, a figure emerged. Monsieur Duval! My breath caught in my throat. He was real. His gaze lingered on me. He looked surprised, maybe even a little disappointed, as he took me in. An itchy feeling spread over my body. Who was he? Just a performer? Or something else?

"I am Philippe Duval, the master of ceremonies, for this, the Circus of Marvels and Wonders." His voice, low and melodic with a touch of a French accent, was captivating. He tapped the silver-tipped walking stick on the wooden stage. It was the same one as in my dream. "Or maybe you won't think it's so curious. Maybe you'll think it's exactly where you belong." He looked right at me, then stretched his arms wide. Just like in my dream, I caught a glimpse of an ankh tattoo at his wrist. "Our show will astound and confound. You will leave wanting more, desperate to become part of this, our eternal show of shows!"

I glanced at Max, who had a small smile on his lips. I relaxed a little. What was the worst that could happen? I was in a public place, and Kris was nearby. I should just enjoy the show.

Monsieur Duval spoke again. "And now, our first act: Concetta, the limbless woman. Be amazed as you watch what this beautiful woman can achieve using only her mouth!" He winked and left with a swish of coattails.

The little man from the front entrance pushed a wheeled dress form into the middle of the stage. On it sat a woman who looked like a real-life armless, legless mannequin. Her skin shone white under the lights, and her hair was curled in tight, springy ringlets, like a cherub. She was so still, she could have been a doll. The little man returned with an easel and positioned it so the pad of paper that sat on it faced the audience.

"Thank you, Leopold," she said to him. Then she turned to us. "I am Concetta, the limbless woman. I have taught myself to do all sorts of things in the absence of my arms and legs." She gazed out at us. I was struck by how pretty she was, with her bright-red lips and perfect skin. "For instance, I will draw one of the members of the audience."

Concetta bent her head down and picked up a pencil on the easel's edge. Holding it in her mouth, she drew; an image came to life on the paper. With the bobbed hair and dramatic eye makeup, there was no doubt who it was supposed to be. "It's you!" Max whispered.

Concetta's eyes fell on me, and she began to quietly sing in Italian. The whispered notes filled my head. It was familiar, but I didn't know how that was possible.

When she was done singing, her face lit up with a smile. Monsieur Duval took to the stage once again, and the little man, Leopold, wheeled Concetta off.

"Ah, beautiful, Concetta," Monsieur Duval said. The music changed to something more exotic. "And now, Ahmed, Noodle Man of the Ganges, will leave you wondering if he has any bones at all."

A man appeared, so skinny I could count his ribs, wearing a leotard and a turban. He reached his hands over his head and twisted them behind his back. The next minute, he was on the floor, contorting his legs through his arms and knotting himself together. He walked on his elbows and turned so his face twisted backwards on his neck. He grinned at me. I couldn't resist smiling back. He was like a human elastic band.

Ahmed untangled his limbs, went up into a back-bend, rolled his belly onto the ground, and then flipped his legs over so that one foot landed on each side of his face. He moved his eyes comically from side to side and crab walked offstage as Monsieur Duval returned.

"There is a saying that two heads are better than one." As Monsieur Duval spoke, the conjoined twins I'd seen before came onstage. "Meet Ella and Elvira."

Theirs was a comedy routine. They took turns delivering the punchlines, often making fun of each other.

Next came Daniel. His face was covered in long silky hair, and he wore a suit. Just like me with my skin condition, there was probably a medical condition that explained his hair growth. But instead of hiding it, he had embraced it.

"Daniel, the Dog-Faced Boy, is not what he appears. He looks like a wild thing, but he has the heart and mind of an artist. Listen as he recites a scene from Shakespeare's *A Midsummer Night's Dream*."

What would have been boring were anyone else doing it was fascinating when it was done by a boy who looked like a werewolf. He moved around the stage, completely engrossed in his performance. He gave each character their own voice, and he would have been at home in any theatre company. I couldn't help but applaud when he finished and bowed to us.

Monsieur Duval came back to the stage, and I leaned forward, eager to hear what the next act would be. "Our final performer will leave you astounded. I am pleased to introduce the jaw-dropping magic of Yuri!"

A man with pale skin and white hair came onto the stage. He was an albino. His white skin, completely devoid of any pigment, made him look ethereal. "Monsieur

Duval flatters me," he began. "I am not so special." He had a Russian accent. "But I do know that if I do this —" he opened his palm, and a butterfly flew out "— you will smile."

I laughed, actually. He went through a series of card tricks, pulling things out of his sleeves and doing the odd clumsy pratfall that turned into a somersault. None of it was astounding, though; it felt like a grandfather performing tricks to make kids laugh. At the end, he pointed at me. "Do you have a bag?" he asked. I nodded. It was lying on the floor at my feet. "Open it, please."

I did as he asked and gasped. The butterfly from the beginning of his show flew out.

Monsieur Duval returned once more. "That is our show," he said with a flourish. "I hope we entertained you with our offering. Perhaps we will see you again." I started to clap, then realized that I was the only one applauding. Max and I were still the only audience members.

We walked down the aisle, and Max held aside the curtains. We were immediately engulfed by the bright lights and noise of Comicon.

"What do you think?" Max asked.

I wasn't sure what I thought. The magical feel of the tent had distracted me from the fact that what I'd been watching was, essentially, a freak show. The performers weren't onstage because they were especially talented, but because they each had a rare physical condition. People were willing to pay to see these "deformities." A show like that might have been okay a hundred years ago, but nowadays, we knew better. Talk about politically incorrect. Then there was the added layer of my own freakishness, which Max didn't know about. The thought of parading around onstage and showing off my skin to anyone who wanted to gawk at it made my stomach turn.

Before I could say any of this to Max, Leopold appeared. "Hey, can we talk to Monsieur Duval?" I asked him.

Max shot me a look. "What are you doing?"

"Don't you want to find out how we know him?"

Leopold hesitated before answering. "Unfortunately, Monsieur Duval is already engaged. Can I pass on a message?"

"It'll just take a second," I insisted. I'd found him — now I needed to figure out who he was.

"Perhaps at our next show," he suggested. "Ella and Elvira, tell this young lady about tomorrow's performance." He gestured to the conjoined twins, who stood in front of the empty ticket booth, then he disappeared back behind the curtains.

"Did you enjoy the show?" one of the twins asked. Their faces were made up identically, like dolls, with dark curls slicked to their foreheads and red lipstick painted in heart shapes on their lips. She didn't wait for me to answer before giving me a handbill. "Here," she said quietly, like she was sharing a secret with me. "You might want this." *Circus of Marvels and Wonders* was emblazoned across the top. "It's for our show tomorrow night. This was just a teaser." She arched an eyebrow at me and smiled. "We hope you'll come."

"Thank you," I said. The one on the right — Ella, I think — winked at me. Then they disappeared behind the curtained area, as well. A few people wandered past and paused, but no one ventured up to the ticket booth. A *Closed* sign had been propped up in the window. Maybe we'd seen their only show of the day.

"Are you going to go?" Max asked, nodding at the handbill.

"I don't know. Maybe." I stuffed it in my jacket pocket. It would give me the chance to talk to Monsieur Duval, find out why he kept popping up in my dreams.

The noise of Comicon drowned out any other thoughts. A T-shirt vendor caught my eye. So did Wonder Woman. "Kris!" I called. She turned.

"Where have you been?" She opened her eyes wide with exasperation. "I've been texting you." Her eyes shifted to Max.

"Sorry. We were at a show. Over in the back corner." I looked in the direction we'd come from, but the aisle had filled up with attendees. "Kris, this is Max. A kid from school." I was bursting to tell her the news. "You're not going to believe this, but the guy from my dream, Monsieur Duval, he was part of the show!"

Kris's eyebrows shot up. "You're kidding! He's real?"

I nodded.

"Let's talk about it over dinner. Wonder Woman is starving. Should we eat here? Or grab a burger somewhere else?"

Kris glanced at Max and back at me, a silent *Should we invite him?* on her face.

"Are you hungry?" I asked him.

He shuffled, looking at his feet. Typical avoidance behaviour. When you're used to the opposite, kindness from strangers can sometimes be the hardest to handle. Been there, done that. "No, thanks."

I didn't push it. I barely knew the kid. Maybe he had friends to meet up with, although judging by the way he'd glommed on to me, I doubted it.

"Are you ever coming to school again?"

His mouth twisted in a scowl. "I don't know."

"How can I get a hold of you?"

He looked taken aback, like it was a question he hadn't been expecting.

"What's your number?" I said.

He shook his head.

"You don't have one?" I guessed. He nodded. "Email?" I asked, although I knew that was doubtful as well. "Okay, look, here's my number." I pulled a pen out of my bag and grabbed for his palm. "Call me if you come back to Henderson —"

That was as far as I got before I broke off. Under the sleeve of his hoodie, his arm was tattooed with a black ankh. The same one Monsieur Duval had.

6

I STARED AT THE TATTOO and then looked at Max. He looked as stunned as I was. He ripped his arm away from me and took off, dashing into the crowd, pushing people out of his way. I stood rooted to the spot, too shocked to move.

"What was that about?" Kris asked.

The noise and the jostling were getting to me. I wanted to be somewhere I could think. "Kris, can we just go home?"

My mind cleared once we were outside in fresh air. It had gotten cooler, and I hunched under my leather jacket, buffeted by the wind. "You must be freezing," I said to Kris.

"Yeah," she agreed with a shiver. "Let's take a cab." She gestured to a few lined up half a block down the sidewalk.

I climbed into the taxi. Kris followed and slammed the door shut. She gave the driver our address and settled in, wrapping her cape around her arms. "How do you know Max?" she asked.

"He showed up at school last week, but only came to a couple of classes. He hasn't been back since. It was weird to see him here."

Kris was quiet for a minute. "And his tattoo? Did that mean something to you?" I knew by her voice that Kris the Trauma Counsellor was springing into action. She might be dressed as Wonder Woman, but my shocked reaction had made her Spidey sense tingle. "Is it something from before?"

Before was shorthand for before I'd been found. The black hole of time that was my childhood.

I shook my head. "It's not that," I told her. "Max's tattoo matches the one Monsieur Duval has."

Kris pulled her cape tighter around her arms.

"Maybe I have ESP," I suggested, sort of joking. "The show felt kind of familiar, too." I thought back to Concetta's song and the atmosphere inside the tent.

I pulled the handbill out of my pocket and looked at it more carefully. The title, *Circus of Marvels and Wonders*, was in that same old-fashioned typeface. Under it was the location and time: *Sunday, 11:00 p.m., Mitchell Ave. Warehouse.* On the bottom left was a drawing of Monsieur Duval in his top hat and tails. He was holding out his arm in a welcoming gesture. The ankh tattoo completely visible. Seeing it sent a shiver up my spine. Kris glanced over. "What's that?"

"Just a handbill." I started to fold it, but she reached over and grabbed it.

"Why are you acting funny?"

"I'm not."

"You are. You're jumpy." I heard the suspicion in

her voice. One thing we'd agreed on before I moved in was complete honesty. When I'd asked her if she was gay, she'd said yes. When she'd asked me about drugs and sex, I'd told her the truth. No to the sex, and mostly no to the drugs.

So why did I lie about this stupid handbill?

Kris scanned it. "That's the same as Max's, isn't it?" she asked, pointing to Monsieur Duval's tattoo. When I nodded, she frowned. "I thought so," she murmured.

"What's that mean?" I asked. Now *she* was the one hiding something.

"Take the next left," she directed the cab driver. "We're third on the right."

"Kris?" I prompted. She couldn't act mysterious and leave me hanging.

"I'll tell you when we get home."

"Tell me now."

"No. Be patient, Frankie."

Patient for what? She gave me back the handbill, and I stuffed it into my pocket.

"I'm going to change," Kris said as soon as we got into the house. Her Wonder Woman cape flapped behind her as she made her way down the hall.

"What did you want to tell me?" I called after her.

"Let me change first."

I heard the metal drawer of the filing cabinet she kept in her room clang shut. She came out of her room a few minutes later, looking serious. In her hands she carried a bulging file folder.

The File.

"No, Kris." I shook my head before she'd even said anything.

"You should see what's inside."

"I don't want to!" My heart started to race. Everything I'd been running from was stored in those papers. All the hurt and abuse. The terror. Foster Moms #1 and #2 each had their chapters in the sordid papers. There were doctors' reports about my skin condition and police reports about all my transgressions. Like a fingerprint, the File had followed me around ever since I'd gone into care.

"I'll be right beside you," Kris said, using her calm voice.

I shook my head. "No!" A rage was brewing — I could feel it tingle in my fingers. A roaring started between my ears. It would explode into my whole body and I'd lose control. I fought against it, taking deep breaths.

"Frankie," she said calmly, firmly. "It's time. This is all in your past. None of it can hurt you anymore. Don't you want to know about the night you were found?"

"I *want* to know, but I'm scared," I whispered through clenched teeth. All these years, I'd pushed that night into the furthest reaches of my mind, burying it so I wouldn't have to think about it. Opening the File now pushed it right in front of me.

"There are more than just reports in here." Kris sat down slowly. Her eyes didn't leave my face.

"Why are you doing this to me?" I asked her.

She licked her lips and pulled out a photo. "The ankh you were talking about — did it look like this?"

It was a polaroid of an ankh pendant hanging off a silver chain. The bottom of the ankh ended in a point.

As quickly as the rage had come, it left, and curiosity filled that space. I reached for the photo.

"The necklace is in here, too." Kris pulled out a plastic evidence bag. A tarnished silver chain pooled at the bottom of it.

"Where did you get this?" I asked. "Why is it in the File?"

She rifled through the papers and pulled out another photo. I gulped. A little girl, hair matted and dirty, in a T-shirt and filthy jeans. Her skin was scaled and flaking. Against her chest lay the ankh. "You were wearing it when they found you." She showed me another photo. Me again, but in this one, I was scrubbed clean and sitting in a hospital room. I was in a different outfit, sitting on a bed with a doll. I remembered that doll. I hated dolls, and I'd hated that one especially. I'd cut her hair and coloured on her face with markers when I got to Foster Mom #1's. The pain and confusion of those first years flooded back.

"Do you want to look at it?" Kris asked, opening the plastic zipper on the top of the bag. I recoiled.

"No, I don't —"

But it was too late. She'd already pulled the chain from the bag, and now the ankh dangled in front of me. "Do you remember it?"

Seeing it sway, the point at the bottom sharp as a dagger — all of it felt familiar. I reached out a finger to trace the shape. It looked just like Monsieur Duval's tattoo and the matching one on Max's arm. What if the ankh was the clue I needed to figure out how we were all connected?

Deep in my gut, I knew the ankh would change things. Even as I touched it, I felt its power rattle through me.

7

I LEFT THE ANKH ON THE TABLE, within reach of my fingertips. My eyes kept darting to it as I considered what would be waiting for me in the File.

The night I'd been found was a hazy memory. I remembered the flashing lights of the police car and chips of glass cracking under someone's shoes. A soft, worried voice had tempted me out of the dark with the promise of food, but I'd been too scared to take it.

They'd asked me my name, where my parents were. I'd stared at them blankly. I was unable to give them any answers — the information they wanted was already locked away in my mind — so I stayed mute. Eventually, they called Kris, a social worker who was an expert in child trauma. She arrived on the scene and spoke to me quietly, calming me. We went to the hospital. Doctors saw me and then detectives tried to piece together who I was. Kris stayed by my side the whole time. Everything they'd discovered since I'd surfaced was in the File that lay on the table in front of me.

"Ready?" Kris asked. I'd resisted reading it before, worried about what it would dredge up. I looked at her, blinking back my fear. It was like opening Pandora's box. "You can't run from it forever, Frankie."

I looked at her, suddenly exhausted. "Why not?"

"It's the only way you'll be able to heal."

"What if I'm not strong enough to handle what I find out?" I whispered.

"You are," she said confidently. "You've come a long way. I wouldn't suggest this if I didn't think you could handle it." She paused, waiting for me to consent. Finally, I nodded, but didn't pull the File closer to me. "Do you want me to read it to you?" she asked.

As Kris read the report from the first cop on scene, some of the hazy memories came into focus. The feel of the cop's hand closing over my arm. He hadn't been trying to hurt me, but I'd clawed and bitten like a wild thing. My shrieks had echoed off the brick walls of the alley. I'd thrashed and gone wild in the back of the car, hammering the windows to be let out. There'd been blood. My own? I touched the dagger-sharp point of the ankh. It could do damage if it had to.

"They took you to the hospital. Children's Emerg," Kris read, showing me the doctor's notes. "You were malnourished and dehydrated. There was a nasty cut on your head, but it was too late to stitch it."

I ran a finger along my hairline. Just above the scales on my right temple was a one-inch scar. The skin was bumpy there where it had knit itself together.

"They suspected you had a concussion, but they couldn't be sure. It would explain the memory loss. They thought you might have been held somewhere. There was bruising on your wrists." Kris's voice dropped. "There was no evidence of any sexual trauma." She gave me a reassuring look before continuing. "And then there's a note about your skin." She flipped to the next page and pulled it out of the File, laying it on the table. "This is a report from Dr. Barbara. Do you remember her? The psychiatrist from the Adolescent Treatment Centre?"

"No." I wasn't enjoying this walk down memory lane. Kris was being as gentle as she could, but each time she flipped to a new document, my stomach clenched. What horrors lay on that page? My past was filled with ticking time bombs, and much of it was a mystery, even to me.

"Do you remember anything else from that time?" The way Kris looked at me, I knew she wanted me to. "You were at the treatment centre for six months. In a private room. You were Frances Doe by then, but I called you Frankie. Frances felt so old fashioned." Kris smiled. "I came to visit you. We'd look outside at the garden. It was fall, and the leaves were changing."

I shook my head, but then a flash of orange and red leaped into my head. "There were squirrels."

"Yeah! You'd watch them jumping from branch to branch for hours. It was the first time I saw you smile."

"I remember you sitting with me," I told her.

"I'd come after work and stay until the nurses kicked me out, or you fell asleep. You'd often mumble just as you were drifting off. I'd write down what I could make out." She showed me her notes — nonsense, even to me. *Fire. Screaming. Run.*

"I don't remember a fire."

"And there weren't any signs of smoke inhalation, nothing that would indicate you'd been in a fire."

As she spoke, I fingered the ankh, running the tip along my thumb. There was something ominous about it.

"I always thought that was a strange piece of jewellery for a little girl to be wearing. I wondered if you'd found it in the alley."

I shrugged. I didn't have any answers.

"The dreams you're having now, they might be your way of working through what happened to you as a child. Suppressed memories or something." Kris frowned. "If you want, we could schedule some therapy sessions. The dreams might be your mind's way of saying it's ready to sort things out."

I looked at her. She knew what my answer would be. I shook my head.

She put the File on the table and pushed it toward me. "It's possible the reason your parents never came forward was because they'd been killed. With your memory loss, it would make sense for you to have witnessed something horrific. Maybe it's finally surfacing."

"But the police —"

"I know. There's no evidence that that's what happened. It's a just a gut feeling." Kris took a deep breath and put her hand on my wrist. "What if whoever hurt your parents came back and threatened you? Maybe that's why you don't want to remember. Your mind is protecting you." She was right. Part of me, a big part, didn't want to remember anything about the past because I had no idea what was lurking back there. But how long could I run from it? First the dreams, then Comicon, and now the File. Maybe escaping my past wasn't an option anymore.

"But it's Monsieur Duval I'm dreaming of. Do you think he had something to do with what happened to me?"

As I said his name, a memory flashed in my head. I was in the hospital room. It was quiet. I heard the door open and shut, and when I turned, someone was there, sitting beside me on the bed.

I frowned, trying to pull out more of the memory. "When I was in the hospital, someone came into my room. A man. He told me not to scream."

Kris leaned forward, eager to hear more. "What did he look like?"

I shut my eyes. "I don't know. It was dark. I was scared. Or maybe just startled because I wasn't expecting anyone. He said he had to tell me something. He sat on the bed and —" I broke off. A horrible chill ran up my spine. "Oh my god, Kris, it was Monsieur Duval! That's how I know him."

Kris nodded for me to go on. "Think, Frankie. What did he tell you?"

I closed my eyes again, squeezing them shut. "He wanted to say sorry. Something had happened and he felt bad. He wished things had been different."

He'd reached out to stroke my hair, but hesitated. *May I?* he'd asked. His fingertips were cool, soothing, as they ran along my forehead, carefully avoiding the bandage. *One day, when you're older, I'll explain things. All of this will make sense. Until then, you must keep all of this a secret.*

What secret had he meant? Who was Monsieur Duval to me?

"Frankie?" Kris prompted. "What else?"

"He told me he'd come back when I was older."

She gave me a long look. "Are you afraid of him? In your dreams, or when you saw him today?"

I thought carefully. "No, not afraid." I searched for

the right word to describe it. "Curious. It's like I'm drawn to him."

Kris reached for my hand and gave it a squeeze. "We'll figure this out," she said.

I nodded, wishing I could be as certain.

I sat on my bed with the contents of the File laid out around me. Kris had gone to sleep a while ago, but I was still up, trying to make sense of things. Now that I'd seen the File, I realized Kris had been right. It wasn't as horrible as I'd imagined. The things the doctors had written, their diagnoses and notes, told me what I already knew.

But the ankh was a mystery. I picked up the photograph of myself when I'd been found. The ankh hung like a weight on my scrawny body. The police report listed where I'd been found. I put the location in my phone, and a red pin appeared on a map of a not-so-nice part of town. Mostly warehouses and factories, it wasn't the sort of place you'd expect to find a little girl wandering alone.

I zoomed in on the alley and noticed a familiar street name. Mitchell Avenue.

Scrambling over the papers strewn across my bed, I dug through my jacket pocket for the handbill from Ella and Elvira. The performance tomorrow night was at a warehouse on Mitchell Avenue. Coincidence?

I pulled the ankh out of the evidence bag and put it on my night table. It was my only belonging from before, assuming I hadn't just picked it up in the alley. What did it mean? And what were the chances of being found wearing the same symbol that was tattooed on Max *and* Monsieur Duval?

The list of questions I had for Monsieur Duval was growing. I folded the handbill in half and put it back in my pocket. There was only one way to get the answers I wanted.

8

MY EYES FLEW OPEN WELL BEFORE I needed to wake up. A new dream of Monsieur Duval was fresh in my mind.

Outside my door, floorboards creaked. The hall light went on. "Frankie?" Kris rapped softly on my door. "Are you awake?"

"Yeah. Just now."

Kris opened the door and peeked her head in. The hall light illuminated my room, which was small and a mess. Like always. Clothes were everywhere except the closet or the drawers. Kris never cared, though. I kept the rest of the house tidy, so my room was my own domain. There was one window behind my bed; it faced the garage in the back. Somewhere under the piles of clothes were a desk and a dresser.

"You were talking in your sleep again."

Kris didn't usually see me without my makeup. That was the first thing I thought of, which was stupid. She knew more about me than anyone in the world, but I still cringed at the thought of her catching me with my skin exposed. I pulled the blanket up to my neck and finger combed my hair forward so it covered my cheeks.

"What was I saying?"

"I couldn't make it out."

"I dreamed about him again." I paused, remembering. "But it was nice." I'd been lying on a pillow, and someone was humming a familiar tune. I knew the notes and could have hummed along, but I'd been too content. A hand stroked my hair, smoothing it off my face, and I fell into blissful contentment, as if this were the only place in the world I was meant to be. "Good night, my sweet angel," a man's voice whispered in my ear. As he moved toward the door, his shadow grew on the wall. The top hat was unmistakable. The man was Monsieur Duval.

"That's good." Kris nodded. Her hand stayed on the doorknob as if she knew I wanted to keep some distance between us.

"Why are you awake?" I asked.

"I was thinking about the File. I shouldn't have pushed you."

"It's okay."

She frowned, unconvinced.

"I don't want to talk to anyone. But if I did, I'd talk to you."

"Okay." The hallway light was on behind her, so I couldn't see her face, but I knew she was disappointed. More than anything, she wanted to help me. She'd broken a lot of rules when she'd asked to foster one of her clients. After what happened with Foster Mom #2's boyfriend #3, Kris said she'd had it with "the system" and wasn't going to let me be victimized again.

"I know you're doing your thing — trying to fix me."

"Not fixing you. That makes it sound like there's something wrong with you, and there's not. It's just hard to see you hurting ..." Kris trailed off. Her concern was keeping us both awake. I yawned.

She took the hint and shut the door. The light in the hallway clicked off.

But when I tried to go back to sleep, I couldn't. I tossed and turned and finally sat up and turned on the light again. I dug through my nightstand drawer for a pencil and propped my sketchbook up on my legs. Drawing was the only thing that made me feel completely at peace. Even drawing something disturbing put my mind at ease. The ankh was different. As it came to life on the paper, I knew there was more to it. The ankh was part of something bigger.

It was time to figure out what that was.

9

I DIDN'T WANT TO LIE TO KRIS ABOUT GOING to the warehouse show, so I didn't. I knew her well enough to know she'd take her usual Sunday night bath. With a glass of wine in hand, she'd run the water so hot that steam fogged up the mirrors and sometimes escaped under the door. She always went in at about nine and emerged, pink-skinned, forty-five minutes later, giddy from the heat and the wine. Then she went straight to bed to gear up for another week at work.

I planned my departure to coincide with her bath. As soon as I heard the water running, I grabbed my bag and slipped the ankh over my head. The weight of it felt leaden, and the chain dug into my neck. I checked that the handbill was still in my jacket pocket and that I had the location of the Mitchell Avenue warehouse on my phone. The Google map did nothing to calm my nerves. Sitting on an isolated stretch of industrial land near the river, the location probably had no streetlights and not a soul nearby to help if I needed it.

I grabbed my pocket knife, too. It was small enough to nestle in the palm of my hand. I left Kris a note on the kitchen table. *Gone out. I'll be careful.* And then I added, *I promise.*

When I first moved in, Kris had set some ground rules. She'd said she wouldn't give me a curfew. She knew trying to keep me under lock and key was the fastest way to never see me again. I could come and go as I pleased, but if she ever wanted to know where I'd gone and who I'd been with, I had to tell the truth. "Just covering my butt," she'd told me. "And yours, too." She didn't always like what I told her about the risk taking and the shady places I found, but I'd never lied. Lately, my need to wander hadn't been as strong as it used to be. I hadn't gone out like this in months, maybe since before the summer.

But the ankh and the dreams had stirred things up in me. I knew that if I told her where I was going, she'd want to come. I couldn't explain why, but finding the Circus of Marvels and Wonders was something I had to do alone.

Anyway, Kris had told me about lots of stuff she'd done when she was young. Sleeping on a beach in some place called Ibiza, hitchhiking through the Rockies. I was young, I was supposed to do stuff like this.

I left quietly, shutting the door carefully so Kris wouldn't hear. I checked the transit app on my phone. A bus would be arriving in a few minutes. In the sky, the moon hung low and large, like a giant eyeball. It was about a week away from being full. I walked to the bus stop and waited, bouncing on my toes to keep warm.

The bus driver gave me a quick look in the rear-view mirror when I stood up at my stop. Just as I'd suspected, it was deserted and dark, without even a streetlight. "You sure this is where you want to get off?" he asked.

No.

"Yeah. I'm meeting someone," I lied. I tried to sound confident, but my stomach churned as I stepped onto the gritty sidewalk, which wasn't actually a sidewalk, but a strip of cement, cracked and strangled with weeds. As the bus pulled away, I thought about running after it and banging on the doors to be let back in.

But the dreams of Monsieur Duval and the information in the File had stirred up questions. I took a deep breath and reminded myself this wasn't the scariest place I'd ever been. An unasked-for image of Foster Mom #2's Boyfriend #3's leering face popped into my head. I gritted my teeth, pushed him away and pulled out the handbill. The paper crinkled when I unfolded it. I looked once more at the drawing of Monsieur Duval and the ankh on his arm. It was an exact match to the pendant. Kris was right that I couldn't hide from my past forever. Was this place going to give me answers?

I slowed down when I got to the spot I'd located on my phone: the alley where I'd been found. It was an alley like any other. The moonlight cast shadows from a dumpster and some broken pallets. Nothing about the alley stood out for me. No memories flooded back. I breathed a sigh of relief. Maybe this whole adventure would be a bust.

Mitchell Avenue was a dead-end street around the corner. I gripped the knife in my pocket, but there was no one around; the place was deserted. There were so few buildings on the street that it was easy to figure out which one was the warehouse. Surrounded by a chain-link fence, the old brick building looked abandoned. Most of the windows were broken, and it was covered in graffiti tags.

I checked the time on my phone. It was almost ten o'clock. Okay, so I was early. That might explain why no one was around. But there weren't any signs to draw people in. From where I stood, I couldn't see any lights on inside the warehouse, either.

I stood outside of the fence, trying to decide what to do. I knew going in was a bad idea, but how else was I going to get answers? The Circus of Marvels and Wonders was probably a travelling show, like all the Comicon exhibits. I didn't know how long they'd be in town, or if they'd ever come back again. This might be my only chance.

I walked around the perimeter of the fence, checking for an entrance. When I found it — a padlocked chain looped through the posts — I almost laughed out loud. Okay, there was no point to being here. I turned to go, mocking my own foolishness. *Who follows a handbill to a deserted part of town? Idiot.*

Somewhere, a door slammed. I spun around and stared at the building. No one was there. I walked closer to the fence, peering through one of the wire diamonds. At the top of the fire escape was a grey metal door. It was shut, but there was a mark on it that I could just make out in the moonlight.

The ankh.

I *was* supposed to be here.

I went back to the padlocked entrance and pushed on the gate, and the chain fell away. It hadn't been properly locked. Slipping through the opening, I walked straight toward the fire escape and grabbed hold of the rusty metal railing.

I paused for a second at the bottom. I was turning into the clichéd girl in the horror movie who runs straight upstairs to where the killer is hiding, instead of outside to safety. But I couldn't help myself. I needed to know what was behind the door.

The fence rattled behind me. My hand went instantly to the knife in my pocket. I spun around. A hooded figure slid through the opening the same way I had and jogged toward me. I opened my mouth to tell the person to back off, when he pulled his hood back.

"Max?" I almost laughed with relief. "What are you doing here?"

"I came to find you."

"How'd you know I'd be here?"

He gave me a sheepish smile. "I didn't know. I guessed. I knew you wanted to talk to Monsieur Duval and that this might be your only chance."

I had to admit, I was happy not to be going into a creepy warehouse alone. Still, I kept my guard up. "That was another nice disappearing act you pulled at Comicon."

"Yeah, sorry about that."

He didn't offer any other explanation. I held out my hands, exasperated. "Your tattoo?" I pressed. "In my dream Monsieur Duval has the same one."

He shook his head. "I don't remember getting it."

I gave him a look of disbelief. Tattoos hurt. How could he forget getting one?

"I'm serious. There's a lot I don't know. I don't know how old I am or how I got here, either. I don't know where my family is, or if I even have one. Everything that happened before a few years ago is a big blank."

I tried to keep my face still, but inside I was trembling. I knew exactly what that felt like.

His pulled his eyebrows together and dug his hands into his pockets. "I registered at Henderson because a couple of weeks ago I saw you going in there. I can't explain it, but I felt like I was supposed to find you."

At any other time, I would have accused him of stalking me, but I knew what he meant. He was familiar to me, too.

"I lied to you at school," Max said. "When you asked me who Monsieur Duval and I are looking for in the dream, I said I didn't know. But that's not true. We're looking for a girl. Her name is Frances."

A buzzing sound like static filled my head. All at once it hit me. When the Monsieur Duval in my dreams asked if *he* had found me, the person he meant was Max.

10

"**A**T SCHOOL, WHEN YOU CALLED ME FRANCES, was it on purpose?"

"I wanted to see what you'd do, if you knew the name. And when I saw the look on your face, it freaked me out."

"In your dreams, why are you looking for her?" I asked. "What's the connection? And why is Monsieur Duval helping both of us?"

A shadow passed over Max's face. "I don't know."

"And your tattoo. And this" — I held up the ankh pendant. Max's eyes widened behind his glasses.

"Where'd you get that?"

"Kris said I was wearing it when they found me."

"What do you mean, when they found you?"

I'd never told my history to anyone who wasn't being paid to help me. Even therapists — besides Kris — had only gotten half truths. But I'd come here for answers, so I needed to come clean with Max. I took a deep breath.

"I was about ten … at least, that's how old they thought I was. I was found close to here. In an alley. I couldn't remember anything. They thought it might be amnesia. Maybe from a concussion or something."

"What about your parents?"

"They tried to find them, but no one came forward."

Max digested this information and nodded. "It was sort of the same for me. I woke up one day in a hotel room. There was food and some clothes. A bag had *Max* written on it, so I figured that was my name. After a few days, the hotel owner started coming around asking to be paid, so I took off."

"Where have you been since then?"

"All over. I crash where I can. There's kind of a crew of kids I hang with downtown. Sometimes we find a place — the park, or a shelter." He was trying to give off an air of toughness, but I saw through it. No kid wanted to live on the street. They did it because they didn't have any other options.

I glanced at my phone. It was getting closer to eleven o'clock. I looked up at the warehouse door. It was still shut, but the ankh told me we were in the right place. "What do we do? There's no one else here," I said. "Just like at the Comicon show."

"Maybe there's another way in," he suggested.

"There's an ankh on that door," I said.

Neither of us made a move.

"Are you scared?" Max asked. I thought about it. The show we'd seen at Comicon had been harmless aside from the weirdness of its being a freak show. "Cuz I am," Max blurted. "I'm crapping my pants, to be honest. We're in the middle of nowhere."

His candour made me laugh. "Yeah, okay. I'm not

super excited about being here, either." But the pull for answers was too strong for me to leave.

"At least we have each other, right?" he said.

I nodded. "Yeah. There's that."

I wasn't sure what a kid who looked twelve was bringing to the table, but I had a knife in one pocket and my phone in the other. Kris had texted asking if I was okay. I wasn't going to reply, but changed my mind. At least if something happened to me, I thought grimly, she'd know where to look for the body.

We clattered up the metal grates of the fire escape. Three flights up, I looked down. Even from up high, I couldn't see another soul. Maybe Max was right and there was a different entrance, or maybe I'd gotten the date wrong. Or maybe, and this idea gave me a chill, we were the only audience they'd wanted.

But they couldn't have known Max and I would find each other. Unless Max was in on it. I side-eyed him as he moved beside me on the narrow fire escape landing. Could his baby face be hiding a criminal mastermind? But he looked as nervous as I felt.

I waited for him beside the door with the ankh on it. There was no handle, just a lock where a key went. "Should we knock?"

"I guess," he mumbled.

The metal door was cool against my knuckles. We waited. I was about to raise my hand again when there was a sound on the other side of the door. It slowly creaked open.

"Here for the show?" I looked down. It was Leopold from the Comicon show, dressed again in his three-piece suit. His moustache had been waxed so that it stuck out on either side of his face.

I glanced at Max and then tried to peer inside the warehouse. It was too dim to see anything. "Yeah."

"Just the two of you?" Leopold didn't sound surprised. "Follow me."

I hesitated in the doorway, watching him walk down a narrow hallway. I checked my phone. No new messages from Kris.

I took a step forward, and Max did the same. As soon as we were inside, the door shut behind us with eerie finality. I had officially turned into a horror movie cliché.

The passageway was lit by bare bulbs dangling from the ceiling. We followed Leopold to the end of the hallway, which opened into a large room lit by strings of bulbs that met in the centre of the ceiling. We took our seats in chairs halfway back from the stage. It was bigger than the one at Comicon and framed by curtains on three sides.

"Where's the rest of the audience?" I asked.

Leopold smiled at me. "You're the only ones who matter."

I shot him a look, wary now. "Who am I to you?"

He pulled out a pocket watch, checked the time, and snapped it shut. "It's showtime." Tinkling carnival music started in the background. Over it, I could hear shuffling footsteps and people muttering. The performers were taking their places.

I pulled out my phone and pressed record, then stuffed it back in my pocket, letting the top peek out. "Smart," Max whispered beside me.

"Does any of this look familiar to you?" I asked, taking in the ochre colour of the backdrop and the size of the stage. I was already planning how I'd draw it in my sketchbook.

He shook his head. "You?"

"No." The lights dimmed and, from the left side of the stage, Monsieur Duval strode forward. His movements were unmistakable, as was his costume and walking stick. Even before I could see his face clearly, I knew it was him.

Monsieur Duval smiled at me, and his teeth glistened.

"Welcome," he said so quietly I had to lean forward to hear him. "We are so glad you've joined us." His voice trembled with emotion.

"Who are you?" I asked.

He put a finger to his lips. "Shh. Tonight is for you, my dear. All of this is for you."

He looked offstage and said, "Leopold, if you please."

Leopold appeared, pushing an easel on wheels. A piece of red velvet had been draped over it. "I want to introduce you to someone," Monsieur Duval said. "Someone who meant a great deal to me. To all of us." He lifted the velvet cloth. Underneath was a heavy golden frame, and inside the frame was a sepia-toned photograph of a smiling girl. Her blond hair was curled in ringlets. She wore petticoats and a dress tied with a sash at the waist. The photograph looked like it was a hundred years old, but that wasn't what captured my attention. It was her skin. Every inch of it was covered in reptilian scales. My breath caught in my throat.

"Let me introduce Frances."

"Her skin," I murmured. It was the little girl I'd seen in my dreams. The one who met Monsieur Duval onstage.

Max gasped. "That's Frances," he said. "That's the girl I'm looking for."

"Both of you know her," Monsieur Duval said. The bright showman's smile paled as he spoke. "She had the same affliction as you, Frankie. It was what made her one of us."

I was still staring at the photograph when I realized there was no logical way he could know about my skin. It was completely covered with makeup right now. "How do you know about me? Who are you?"

Monsieur Duval took a step toward me. I stood up so abruptly my chair fell behind me. "Don't come any closer," I warned. The old-fashioned piano music that had been playing in the background suddenly stopped.

Monsieur Duval stared at me from the stage and held his hands up, placating. "You misunderstand, Frankie. We just want to talk to you. Give you a choice."

"A choice about what?" I eyed him suspiciously. My panic rose as Ahmed, the contortionist, appeared from backstage, then Daniel the Dog-Faced Boy, and a man so tall he had to stoop so as not to get entangled in the strings of lights. I started to tremble. Max and I were outmatched. The two of us didn't stand a chance against a whole troupe of performers.

"The choice of whether or not you wish to join us," Monsieur Duval said.

"Join you?" I sputtered. "As what? Part of your freak show?" The idea was horrifying. "Oh my god. I need to get out of here." I turned to Max, but he was transfixed by the performers. When he looked at me, his eyes were wide with shock.

All of a sudden, the lights went out, and the room plunged into darkness. A hand grabbed my wrist. I screamed and jerked it away. "It's me!" Max said.

"We have to get out of here."

"Follow me," he said.

He grabbed my hand and took a few steps, but my clunky boots got tangled up in the legs of the chair. With a crash, I fell to the ground.

When I opened my eyes, I wasn't in the warehouse, I was outside in a field, staring down at a boy. And I wasn't me anymore, I was Frances, the girl from the photograph.

11

M Y DRESS. Papa would be mad if I got it dirty. I wasn't supposed to wear good clothes when we weren't performing, but the dress was so much prettier than my plain old calico dresses. I ignored Gus's grimy fingers and the muddy smudges on his face and held up a handkerchief for him to blow his nose on. He always looked — and smelled — in need of a bath. "I won't let anything happen to you," I said again. "I promise." There was a bruise on his cheek.

"He hit me so hard, I blacked out." His eyes welled with tears as he spoke.

I pursed my mouth, stroking his head, momentarily distracted by the way my lizard skin shone. With her gnarled fingertips, Abeline had gently massaged a greasy concoction into my skin, just like Mama used to do. *Mama.* Her name echoed in my head.

I turned my attention back to Gus. "It was an accident," I reminded him. "Papa didn't mean to hurt you. You shouldn't make him angry."

"I don't try to," he pouted. "I didn't mean to spill it."

Gus was a thorn in Papa's side. I'd seen the look that Papa shot at Gus when he didn't deliver water fast enough, or when he tripped over his too-big shoes. Having none of the finesse of a performer, Gus's clumsiness was a constant source of irritation.

"He's always mad at me. I'm not special like you."

This was true, so I didn't argue. I was special. I was Alligator Girl. Papa loved me. The performers adored me. I was their angel. People came from all over to see me. Gus, though, was just a regular boy. But I'd liked the little vagrant as soon as I'd seen him lingering outside the circus, too poor to afford a ticket in. He was a scrawny boy with freckled skin and big green eyes. I'd found him after the shows were over, curled up by a tree. He had nowhere to go, that much was clear, and he didn't say boo, just stared at me like a lost puppy grateful for attention. I'd dragged him to Papa, begging to keep him. I was desperate for a friend, especially since Mama was gone. Papa relented, finally, and called the boy over. Gus approached nervously, looking up at Papa with the eyes of someone used to being trampled on. He'd escaped from a home for boys, he said.

Papa had sighed with irritation. He'd been short-tempered lately, but he didn't often refuse me. "If you give me any trouble, boy, you'll be out. You understand?"

Gus had nodded, but his eyes lit up. "So, I'm part of the show, now? I'll travel with you?"

Papa had snorted. "You'll do as I say. And you're not part of the show. You're not a performer. You're a stable boy. That's your place, and don't forget it." Gus hadn't been deterred by Papa's harsh words. He said it was no worse than he'd been treated before. But I wanted Papa to be nicer to Gus. If his bad temper pushed Gus away, I'd be alone again, just me and all the grown-ups. I'd have no one to play with.

Summoning up my conviction, I looked at Gus now. "I'll talk to Papa."

Gus pressed a palm against his eyes to stop the tears and sat up.

He'd confessed to me that running away with a circus had always been his dream.

I didn't have the heart to tell him that technically, we weren't a circus. We were a carnival side show. Years ago Papa had split from the original circus, preferring to travel on his own, and here we were. He'd reinvented the show lots of times, repainting the name on the wagon each time. *Monsieur Duval's Human Curiosities* had been the last one. But I liked what we were called now best. *Monsieur Duval's Circus of Marvels and Wonders.*

I smoothed out my dress where Gus had laid his grubby hands. "We have a new exhibit arriving tonight, did you hear? All the way from Egypt!" I hoped the distraction would cheer Gus up, make him forget his troubles for now, until I could talk to Papa.

"What is it?" Gus asked.

I drew in a breath and gave a dramatic pause. "A mummy!"

He wrinkled his nose. "A mommy? That's not weird. Who'd come to see a mommy?"

"No, you silly!" I giggled. "Not a mother. A dead Egyptian king all rolled up in bandages. Haven't you heard of King Tut?" It had been all over the news in every city we'd stopped in lately. Papa collected the papers and tacked them up on his board. "He was buried for thousands of years, and a man broke into his tomb and found him! And all his treasure!"

That piqued Gus's interest. "What kind of treasure?"

I didn't really know, but there was no point letting that ruin a good story. "Mountains of gold and diamonds and emeralds and rubies. Even the mummy's coffin was painted in gold!" I'd never seen real jewels, but Tabitha, the bearded lady, wore a necklace of fake rubies that glittered onstage. Real rubies must be even brighter! Imagine digging your hands into a pile of blinding stones in King Tut's tomb.

I leaned close to Gus. "They say that as soon as the men entered Tut's tomb, they were cursed." I made my voice deep and menacing. "Beware! He who crosses into this grave will suffer a fate worse than death!"

Gus's eyes bulged with fear. "What about the mummy we're getting? Is he cursed, too?"

I could have let him off the hook, but it was too delicious to see the look on his face as I spun a yarn.

"Frances!" Papa's voice boomed from behind us. The circle of white circus tents sat just beyond a hill. The red flag on the top of the main tent waved in the breeze. Large canvas screens stretched on wooden frames had been set up around the perimeter — the best we could do to stop people from sneaking in. Each one advertised one of the sights the audience could find inside. The screens met at the front under the large sign with the name of the circus: *Monsieur Duval's Circus of Marvels and Wonders.* Papa had a stage by the ticket seller, and he'd stand up there and shout out the amazing collection of Marvels and Wonders. Inside, there were a few small tents where, for a few extra pennies, people could gain admission to see curiosities. The main tent was in the centre, and that was where each of us performed, delighting the crowd with our talents.

"Maybe the mummy has arrived!"

Gus looked horrified. "Don't go!"

"Frances!"

"Coming, Papa!" He strode to the top of the hill and looked down at us. Papa was the most handsome man I'd ever seen. He could have been in the talkies that Ella and Elvira raved about. Swathes of grey cut into his hair at the temples, and his bronzed skin glowed across his cheekbones. He was Métis. His mother was Cree and his father French. He could speak three languages fluently, and a bit of Polish and Ukrainian, too. Tall and broad-shouldered, he commanded any room with ease and was a natural onstage.

He wasn't in his performing clothes today, just a loose work shirt and pants held up with suspenders. He and the other men had been doing repairs while the women laundered and cleaned, preparing for a weekend of shows. He shot a dismissive look at Gus and held out a hand for me.

Gus hunched his shoulders and stared at the ground. I slipped my hand into Papa's. "Come," he ordered and pulled me to my feet. "And you." He shot Gus a look. "Thor needs help with the horses. You shouldn't be lazing about when there's work to be done."

Gus nodded and stood, walking in the opposite direction from us. I thought about asking Papa to be kinder to Gus, but it was so lovely to have him all to myself. I didn't want to ruin the moment. "Is the mummy here?" I asked.

"Not yet." He grinned, raising an eyebrow. "Soon, though."

I skipped beside him, my blond hair bouncing on my shoulders as we crested the hill overlooking the circle of white tents below.

12

I OPENED MY EYES. Someone was saying my name over and over.

"Frankie?" Max stared down at me. "Are you okay?" He sounded panicked.

"What happened?" Images blended together. I looked around for the tents, but I was in a room, lying on a wooden floor. I remembered the circus. Pushing myself to a sitting position, I realized I was in a warehouse.

"You fell and blacked out."

I sat for a moment, shaking off the blurred line between the dream and reality. The lights were back on, and the chairs that had tripped me up lay in a tangled mess. "How long was I out?"

"Not long. Can you stand?" Max asked. He reached his arms out to me and pulled me to my feet. I turned to the stage, but it was empty. I stood still for a moment, listening. There were no murmurs backstage, nor any footsteps on the creaky floorboards. "Are they gone?"

"I think so."

I took a deep breath and sat down on a chair, resting my head in my hands. There was a pain at my right temple. Gingerly, I felt a lump swelling beside my scar. I hated that I'd been so vulnerable. An unconscious girl in a strange place with a bunch of men ... the idea made me shudder. Anything could have happened.

But other than my head, nothing hurt. I looked back at the stage to the spot where Monsieur Duval had been standing. "He wanted me to join the circus," I said, remembering his words. "He was trying to recruit me."

"He said your skin —"

I nodded. "I have the same thing as Frances. Lamellar ichthyosis is the medical term."

"You wear makeup to cover it?" Max guessed.

I nodded. "I don't know how he knew about my skin, or why he thought I'd want to put myself on display like that."

"Frances did it."

"Yeah," I scoffed. "Well, times have changed." I stood up, but had to hold on to a chair to wait for a dizzy spell to pass.

"I'm still trying to figure out how I'm involved," said Max. "I know Frances is who I'm looking for in my dreams, and Monsieur Duval said I was part of the circus, too. But I'm not special like you."

I sat down again. His words, *I'm not special like you*, echoed in my head. The boy, Gus, had said the same thing in my dream. I tried to pull the hazy images from my mind. "I dreamed about her. Just now, when I hit my head."

"Who?"

"Frances."

Max's eyebrows shot up.

"There was a kid who looked like you. A little, anyway." I looked at Max. There was a resemblance to Gus, but the hair and eyes were different. So was their personality. Gus needed protection, but Max was a survivor. I could see it in his guarded glances and the way he watched the people around him. Living in care did that to a person. You learned to be careful about who you trusted.

"Now you're dreaming about me?" he smirked. I rolled my eyes at him.

"Not just you. Monsieur Duval was there, too." But he hadn't been Monsieur Duval in my dream. He'd been Papa, and I'd loved him.

"I need to call Kris," I said, reaching for my phone. My pocket was empty. I looked at the floor. "My phone," I said. "Did you see it?"

"No." He spun in a slow circle with his eyes on the ground, searching. Together, we pushed chairs out of the way to clear a wider area. "It must have fallen out when you fell," he said. How far could it have gone?

I looked at the front pocket of Max's hoodie and his baggy pants. There was plenty of room to hide a phone. "You mind?" I said and pointed. "Can I make sure it didn't *accidentally* get lost on you."

"Oh." Max nodded. "Yeah. I mean, I don't have it. I'm not an idiot." *No, but you might be a thief.* He shook his hoodie and patted down his pockets to prove they were empty. It didn't really prove he hadn't taken the phone, though. He could have stashed it somewhere.

"It didn't just disappear," I said. "Did anyone come near me when I fell?" Unease twisted through my stomach.

Max shook his head. "No one. When the lights came on, they were gone."

My shoulders sagged at the thought of leaving without my phone. Someone had taken it. Was it him? Or one of the performers?

"At least now you know why Monsieur Duval's interested in you," Max said as we walked toward the exit.

I shot Max a look. "It doesn't explain why he keeps showing up in my dreams. Or why we both have them." I didn't bother to keep the annoyance out of my voice. "I wish I'd never come here," I muttered under my breath.

13

B Y THE TIME WE GOT BACK TO KRIS'S, it was after two in the morning. I held my finger to my lips. "Shh!" I said to Max. I hadn't had the heart to abandon him in the middle of downtown, so I'd told him it would probably be okay with Kris if he crashed on the couch. I left him in the kitchen and went down the hall to Kris's room.

A light flicked on inside and glowed through the crack under her door. "Frankie? You're back." There was relief in her voice, then the rustle of her sheets and blankets as she got out of bed. She opened her door. "I texted you."

Now wasn't the time to tell her I'd lost my phone. "Yeah, it was sort of an eventful night," I said. "Max is here."

"The kid from Comicon?" She went back into her room and threw her bathrobe over her flannel pyjamas.

"He was at the show, too. I didn't feel right about ditching him. I don't think he has anywhere to go. Can he crash here tonight?"

I could tell she wasn't excited about the idea, but it was so late. I knew she wouldn't turn him away. She followed me to the kitchen, where Max was inspecting some photos attached to the fridge with magnets. None were of me.

"Hi, Max," she said, admirably upbeat, considering the circumstances. "I hope the couch is okay."

"Yeah, that'll be fine. Thanks."

"Frankie can get you a blanket —" She stopped and narrowed her eyes. "What's that?"

I touched the spot on my head that she was staring at. "It's nothing. Just a bump."

"What happened? Did you fall?"

"Sort of. Maybe you should sit down." Now Kris was really worried. Her eyes flicked between me and Max. I pulled out a chair to sit, and Max and Kris did the same. "When we got to the show, Monsieur Duval was there. He acted like he knew me. I know it sounds bizarre, but I think Max and I are connected through him."

Kris frowned. "How?"

I took a deep breath. "When we got there, to the show, Monsieur Duval showed us a photograph of a girl. She had skin like mine. Her name was Frances." Beside me, Max nodded. "It freaked me out, and when I stood up, I tripped and hit my head. I was out cold for a while, and I had another dream … but this time it was more like a memory. I saw things through Frances's eyes. Monsieur Duval was in the dream, and so was a kid named Gus."

Kris raised her eyebrows. "Did you talk to Monsieur Duval — the real one, not the one in your dream — and find out what he wants?"

"Yeah. He wants me to join his circus."

I didn't think it was possible, but Kris's eyebrows rose even higher. "His circus?" she repeated. "Frankie," she said calmly, "don't be offended when I ask this, but were you high?"

"No." I shook my head emphatically.

Kris pursed her lips. "Is it possible someone slipped you something?" She shot a suspicious look at Max. His eyes darted back to the floor.

"No," I said, my frustration mounting. "Besides my head hurting, I feel fine. And Max is as confused about all of this as I am."

"And the tattoo?" She gave Max a pointed look.

"Tell her," I said to him.

"I don't remember getting it," he said.

Kris looked at him as incredulously.

"I don't remember anything. It's like I woke up one day, and it was the first day of my life."

Kris took a deep breath. "Are you guys pranking me?"

"I wish we were," Max said.

"Weird, right?"

Kris slowly nodded at me. "Are you in danger? Does he want to hurt you?"

"No. I mean, he had the opportunity. I was out cold and, no offence" — I gave Max a once-over — "but you're not much of a threat." I tried to put into words how I'd felt when Monsieur Duval had gazed at me from the stage. "It was like he … missed me. But then I got freaked out. He knew stuff, like about my skin, and he started coming closer. You know how I get."

Kris nodded. She rubbed her forehead as she formulated a plan. "First thing tomorrow I'll call one of my cop friends. Maybe they can dig something up on this guy."

"There's one other thing," I said. I may as well confess now instead of waiting until tomorrow. "I lost my phone."

Kris sighed and pulled her own phone out of her bathrobe pocket. "Was the locator on?"

"I don't know," I said. I ignored the annoyed look she shot me.

She dialed my number and held the phone to her ear. "No answer." She put the phone on the counter. "We're not going to get anywhere with this tonight. I'll take you to this warehouse tomorrow to look around, and I'll ask someone to look into this Monsieur Duval guy." She looked at Max. "I'll get you a pillow for the couch."

Once Max was settled on the couch, Kris and I went to our rooms. Before she went inside, she shot me a look and pointedly turned the lock on her doorknob. I nodded and did the same. I changed out of my clothes and into an old T-shirt, then started the laborious process of removing my makeup and then coating my face with a medicated cream.

As always, I inspected my skin in the mirror. Without the heavy foundation to glue it down, pieces of skin flaked off. Underneath, a new layer grew, shiny and pink for the moment. Within days, it would turn dark and crusty, and then I'd shed it. My whole body was like this, some parts more reptilian than others. I pulled off my fingerless gloves and looked at my hands under the harsh glare of the desk lamp.

In my dream, Frances had had skin that shimmered, each scale catching the light. I closed my eyes and pulled as much of the dream from my memory as I could. Frances and Gus had been in a field, with the circus tents in the distance. Before Monsieur Duval arrived, she'd been telling the boy about a mummy.

I went to my nightstand and picked up the ankh necklace. I put my finger under the point, careful not to pierce the skin.

The ankh was an ancient Egyptian symbol associated with everlasting life. I'd paid enough attention in my Ancient Civ class to remember that. And the Egyptians had mummified their dead so that souls could find their bodies again in the afterlife. The two things had to be connected. Maybe Monsieur Duval was part of some cult? That would explain his tattoo. But what about Max's?

And if they'd really wanted me to join them, they could have just kidnapped me. They'd had plenty of opportunity, especially while I was unconscious. Why let me leave?

The laptop Kris and I shared was on my desk under a pile of clothing. I typed in *ankh*. A stream of photos filled the images page. I clicked on one of the pictures and was directed to a Wikipedia page. I scanned it, but didn't find anything new. I went back to the search results page and scrolled farther down, looking for an ankh that ended in a point at the bottom. Hundreds of images later, I found an illustration that looked almost identical to the necklace. I clicked on that image and leaned closer to the screen to read.

The ankh I'd been found with, the one in the tattoos, didn't mean everlasting life. It was a symbol for death.

14

I'D BEEN STARING AT THE COMPUTER for too long, and my eyes burned.

Each click of the mouse led me deeper down a rabbit hole. On the site about the ankh, I'd discovered information about a slew of other Egyptian artifacts, including mummies. From there, I'd started searching for images of circuses. I scrolled through them mindlessly. I knew I should go to bed. The sun would be up soon.

The dreams were taking me back in time. Frances had known about King Tut's tomb, which meant it was sometime after 1923. I searched for *circus, side show* and *freak show 1920s* and was rewarded with more images. Many were of cabinet cards, which were like trading cards used by performers to advertise their acts. I stopped at one sepia-toned image. *Siamese twins Ella and Elvira*, read the cabinet card title. Two women's heads stuck out of one neck. It was the conjoined twins from the Comicon show, I was sure of it. But the photo had been taken in 1918.

My fingers flew across the keys as I typed in another name. Concetta, the limbless woman, appeared in an outfit similar to the one she'd worn on the stage at Comicon. Her photo was black and white, and the stamped date read 1920. I started to sweat. I typed in *Ahmed, Noodle Man of the Ganges*. There he was, grinning at the camera, his moustache curled and his body contorted into a pretzel-like twist, 1921.

I pulled my hands off the keyboard and sat back. This wasn't possible.

I took a deep breath. They could be actors, or LARPers, fans of Live Action Role Play, like the people I'd seen in the park recreating battle scenes from the Middle Ages. Maybe all those people were pretending. There had to be a logical way to explain how someone in a photo from more than a hundred years ago could still be alive today.

I rubbed my eyes again. It was almost three o'clock. I needed sleep.

I closed the laptop and slid it under my bed so I wouldn't step on it. I changed and got ready for bed. My mind was still reeling when I scrunched up the pillow under my cheek, but I was so exhausted that I knew sleep wasn't far away. The ankh was on my nightstand. It was the last thing I saw as I closed my eyes.

Gus and I ducked below the stage. We were off to the side, giggling with excitement. I let him clutch my hand. Papa had told Gus and me that we were not to join the rest of the troupe, not yet. Mr. Hussein, the purveyor of the mummy, had told Papa that children could find the mummy upsetting. I'd begged Papa, but he'd remained firm. I was not to take part in the opening of the crate.

But Gus and I had snuck in, anyway. No one noticed us. We hid at the bottom of the stage and peeked over the edge to take in what we could. Papa gave Thor, our Viking giant and horse wrangler, a crowbar. "You may do the honours," he said in his stage-show voice. Even when he wasn't in his costume, Thor was an intimidating figure. More than seven feet tall with long hair and a red beard, he towered over the rest of us. Thor jammed the crowbar under the lid of the crate and, with a flick of his wrist, pried one corner loose.

Mr. Hussein stood beside Papa. The whites of his eyes shone against his dark skin. He wore a hat with a tassel and a long gown that billowed around his feet. He reminded me of a hawk, with his hooked nose and his eyes that missed nothing. The other performers were wary of him, too. When he'd first arrived, Papa had invited him to eat with us, but his long stares had made everyone uncomfortable.

Concetta had been wheeled out in her special chair by Daniel. The silky hair that covered Daniel's head and face hung down his chest. He put a hand on Concetta's shoulder as she fretted. He tilted his head and gave her a reassuring smile, and then his eyes landed right on me and Gus. I held my finger to my lips. Daniel winked at me and pivoted Concetta's chair so she could see the sarcophagus better without catching sight of us.

The others were there, too, including Ella and Elvira. Ella on the right primped and preened, while Elvira almost toppled them both over when she leaned forward to watch Thor open the crate. Ahmed, wearing his turban and a long robe of embroidered fabric, paced the stage in his bare feet. Shirley, the fat lady, sat on a stool that disappeared under her girth. Fat pooled around her ankles. Abeline, who'd been our four-legged woman before Mama, sat beside Leopold, the dwarf. Abeline was too old to perform now, so she worked as our cook and seamstress. My favourite performer, Yuri, the albino magician, who had been training to be a doctor before he'd joined us, had taken a seat beside Tabitha, the bearded lady.

"What's going on?" Gus asked. I was standing on an overturned crate, but he couldn't see over the floorboards without jumping.

"Find something to stand on," I whispered. "They're going to open it!" I didn't take my eyes off of the stage as Thor removed the lid and the wooden sides of the crate fell away. There was a collective gasp. Mr. Hussein motioned for Thor to stand back. A giant sarcophagus stood on the stage, covered in Egyptian hieroglyphs.

"Today marks a new day for us, my friends," Papa said. "Already, we are like family, but with this antiquity, our lives will be forever linked."

"What does that mean?" Gus whispered.

I gave him an annoyed look. "Hush! I don't know, but we won't find out if you keep talking."

Papa continued. "The gift of this mummy means there will be no fear of the separation of death. Never again will we have to lose one of our own." Everyone bowed their heads, and a hush fell over them.

"Mathilde would have wanted this for us. Unfortunately, it is too late for her." His voice cracked.

Tears filled my eyes. He was talking about Mama. An image of her walking between the tents, her skirt billowing in the breeze, came to mind. I'd run to catch up with her, and she'd smiled, looking at me with a loving gaze. She hadn't been my real mother, just like Papa wasn't my real father, but the three of us were a family. That is, we had been a family.

"But we can go forth. We are the curiosities of the world, my friends. We entertain and delight in our strangeness. We wish no ill upon others, no matter how they may terrorize us."

Heads rose and prayers were murmured. "Is he talking about your mama?" Gus asked. He'd arrived after her time. When Mama died, Papa had been inconsolable, and I'd been relegated to the care of others, a rotating band of nursemaids who'd given me teary smiles and as many sweets as I wanted. They thought I didn't understand what had happened, that affection and penny candies would ease my grief. They had no idea that I'd seen it all. I knew what had happened to Mama.

Whatever question Gus was going to ask died on his tongue as Papa helped Thor to lift the sarcophagus's lid. Everyone held their breath. The seal on the coffin cracked, and there was a hiss of air, as if the coffin were exhaling. "Open it!" squealed Elvira. She and Ella clapped their hands together.

"What can you see?" Gus asked.

I shushed him. "Nothing yet."

"Can we sneak closer? No one's paying any attention."

It was true. All eyes were on what was inside the crate. I nudged Gus to move around the stage to the stairs. As we crept up, he tripped on his own feet and landed on his belly with an "Oof!" I froze stock-still beside the stage, and when I looked up, Papa's eyes were on me. They burned bright with excitement.

15

THE BEEP OF MY ALARM CLOCK pulled me back from Frances's world. I slapped at it to turn it off, and my hand fell on the ankh. Underneath it lay my sketchbook. With my eyes half-closed, I pulled the book toward me and dug a pencil out of the drawer. The story that had unfolded in my dream had felt so real.

It *was* real, I reminded myself. According to my research, those performers had actually existed. Did they still? It sounded impossible, but I'd seen them with my own eyes. So what did that make my dreams? Memories? A past life, maybe?

And what about Max? If I switched out the bleached buzz cut for a shaggy mop of dark hair and got rid of his glasses and piercings, could he be Gus from the dreams?

I flipped open the File and found the photo of myself when I'd been found. My mousy brown hair, wide-set brown eyes, and pointed chin were nothing like Frances's blond curls and blue eyes. The only similarity between us was our skin.

I didn't believe in reincarnation. Part of the beauty of death was that this life would be over. People had it wrong, the way they thought life was the part to be savoured. To me, we had to live in order to die. Morbid? Yes. Welcome to being a goth. I wasn't religious. Maybe heaven existed, I didn't know for sure. I didn't dwell on the spiritual side of things. I knew the ancient Egyptians had, though. They had thought the point of living was to get to the afterlife, where your soul could be free. That was what a real ankh represented: the soul's everlasting life. But, I remembered, the ankh variation I kept coming across meant something else entirely.

What had a ten-year-old orphan been doing with a symbol that meant death? Kris had been right; it was a weird thing for a little girl to be wearing.

I looked at what I'd drawn so far. The story of the circus was coming to life on my page. The first frame in my sketchbook was Gus and Frances crouched under the stage. Only their eyes were visible, and they were wide with childish excitement. The next square showed Monsieur Duval hovering over the crate, a look of glee on his face, a rough layer of stubble over his chin.

He'd stopped shaving after Mathilde's death. The surety of the knowledge caught me off guard. How could I know that?

Kris knocked on my door. "Frankie? Are you awake?" she asked.

"Yes."

"Can I come in?"

"Hang on." I pulled a hoodie over my T-shirt and

tugged the hood around my face before unlocking the door. Only my nose, mouth, and eyes peeked out.

I went to sit back on the bed and pulled the covers over my legs. "Max is gone," she said. "Folded all the blankets, though. Did you hear him leave?"

I shook my head, not surprised. "He's not big on goodbyes."

Kris looked around my room with her familiar frown of semi-disgust, but didn't say anything about the mess. My sketchbook lay on the end of my bed in plain sight. She pulled it closer to get a better look.

"That's quite a cast of characters." I'd drawn them each with as much detail as I could recall. Yuri, the albino; Shirley, the fat lady; Thor, the giant; and Daniel, the hairy man. A separate frame showed Ahmed, Noodle Man of the Ganges; Leopold, the dwarf; Concetta, the limbless woman; and the conjoined twins, Ella and Elvira. In yet another frame, Tabitha, the bearded lady, and wizened old Abeline, the four-legged woman, stood together. Mr. Hussein stood in the background, apart from the rest of the performers.

"Side show freaks," I said quietly.

Or, a family, and Monsieur Duval was the patriarch.

She pointed to the scene where Gus and Frances peered over the top of the stage, their eyes wide with wonder. "Is that Max?" she asked.

"In the dream, his name is Gus. You think they look the same?"

"A little. He looks more innocent," Kris said, pointing to the drawing. "Max has more edge."

Understandably, I thought. A few years on the streets would do that.

"And that's Frances," she murmured.

I nodded. In the drawing, her alligator skin was on full display.

"What's in the crate?" she asked.

"A mummy."

She made a noise in her throat. "Really? What are they doing with it?"

"I don't know yet." I glanced at the ankh on my nightstand.

The aroma of coffee wafted in from the kitchen. "You should get ready for school. I have to go to court, so I can drop you off on the way."

I gave Kris a pleading look. "I barely slept."

"I made the coffee extra strong."

Despite generally moving through school like a shadow, I'd been making an effort this year. I liked Mrs. O'Brian's English class, and Mr. Kurtis was cool. Film studies was easy, and bio — well, it would be a miracle if I squeaked by with 50 percent, but if I kept it up, I might get a few more credits. Graduation was still a long way away, but it wasn't impossible.

Going to school was another one of Kris's dealbreaker rules. She'd said if I wanted to stay here, I had to attend. I'd stomped and shouted, trashing my room in anger. She hadn't wavered. "You can't make me!" I'd said. But I knew where I'd end up if I didn't follow her rules.

Those first few days of high school, I'd felt like I was teetering on a tightrope, the length of it impossible to cross. Everything had been so overwhelming. Kris had told me to take one step at a time. Last year, I'd ended up passing three classes. I'd set a goal this year to pass four. I hadn't told Kris that. I didn't want to get her hopes up. Plus, the thought of telling her I was setting goals seemed so lame.

"Fine," I groaned.

Kris smiled. "Be ready in half an hour."

Compared to other mornings, I'd gone easy on my make-up, or at least the eyeliner. "It might be a long day for me," Kris said as we pulled up to Henderson High. "You can order in for dinner, if you want."

"And miss one of your fine meals?" I asked sarcastically. Kris was the first to admit that she was a terrible cook.

"Ha ha. Careful, or it'll be lentil stew for a week." Her last foray had been a recipe that had looked like gruel and tasted worse.

"Hey," she said as I got out of the car, "if you see Max, let him know if he needs a place to crash once in a while ..."

I grinned at her. She was the queen of giving a kid a chance. "I'll let him know."

I was early for first period. The halls were mostly deserted. A few kids hung around the gym, taking a break from a team practice, and a few others trickled into the library. I didn't bother going to my locker and headed straight for Mr. Kurtis's art room.

"Mind if I work in here?" I asked.

Mr. Kurtis was slugging back some coffee from his *Mediocre Teacher of the Year* mug. "Yeah, no problem."

I sat down and yawned. Even Kris's extremely potent coffee wasn't waking me up.

"Tired?" he asked.

"I didn't sleep much."

"Everything okay?"

I imagined telling Mr. Kurtis about my weekend. How the man I dreamt about was real and ran a hundred-year-old circus. He would have escorted me to the guidance counsellor's office before I could blink. "Long story. It's fuelled some ideas, though."

"Can I take a look?"

I pulled my sketchbook out of my bag and flipped the cover open. His eyebrows shot up when he saw what I'd done. "Whoa. Cool."

I flushed at his reaction.

"Do you have a whole story mapped out?"

"It's unfolding as I go," I said.

"It might be easier if you had a plan for it. You know, a beginning, middle, and end. Is she the main character?" he asked, pointing to Frances.

"Yeah. That's Frances."

I glanced at Mr. Kurtis. He hadn't shaved this morning, and a dusting of stubble covered his chin. I'd never noticed the small scar that ran through his eyebrow, either. With a start, I shifted away from him. If I could see all that, he'd be able to see through my makeup to what lay underneath.

"So, what's her story? Like, is she happy living with this circus — what do you call it?" He flipped back to the first page, where I'd drawn a banner. "The Circus of Marvels and Wonders." He smiled. "Or does she want something more? Maybe travelling around like this is hard for her, and she wants to settle down, make some friends her own age?"

I shook my head. "That's why she has him." Gus stared back from the frame with a boyish grin. He clearly adored his friend.

"Okay," Mr. Kurtis said slowly, "I'll buy that, but she still needs to want something. What's her problem, and what's getting in the way?"

It wasn't Frances's skin, I was sure of that. She was still young. She hadn't learned to be embarrassed about it, not yet, anyway. And she seemed content with the circus; they were her family. "I'm not sure yet," I admitted.

"Give it some thought. Try to inhabit her world as much as you can."

I bit back a wry laugh at that comment. There was movement at the door. The girl from bio who I'd dubbed a wannabe April took a tentative step into the classroom. She looked a bit ragged, too, for an April. "Is the art room open?" she asked. She glanced in my direction, but kept her face neutral. The April-type girls didn't usually hang out in the art room. They hung out in the front hallway on a bench under the trophy case, making sure everyone knew this was *their* school.

And they rarely left their post, so I wondered why this girl wasn't with them.

"You've got work to do?" Mr. Kurtis asked.

She nodded.

"Come on in," he said.

I scowled at her, wishing Mr. Kurtis had told her no, she wasn't welcome here — which, ironically, was very April of me.

But then she picked a desk in the back corner, as far away from me as humanly possible, and pulled out her sketchbook. She propped it up against the edge of the desk and positioned her phone in front of it. She might

have thought she was being sneaky, but it was obvious
she had no intention of drawing. That was one reason
girls like her irritated me. It wasn't just their nasty comments, it was how they thought that because they were
pretty and popular, rules didn't apply to them.

92

16

I RETURNED HOME TRIUMPHANT. I'd survived an entire day at school with very little sleep. Bio had even been fun because we'd gotten to dissect a heart. A pig's heart, not a human heart, which was Mr. Yeng's first joke of the year. I'd been stuck with a squeamish kid who excused himself after five minutes, so I got to do the dissection by myself. There'd been no sign of Max, which wasn't a surprise, but I did find myself thinking about him. After my dream last night, I had a lot of questions.

Kris had left a voice message on the machine. "Hey, Frankie, it's me. I'm going to be home even later than expected. Things kind of blew up with one of my cases. By the way, I asked a cop I know to look into the warehouse, but I haven't heard anything yet. I tried calling your phone a few times, too, but there's still no answer. I'll keep trying in case someone found it. See you later."

A phone was a useful tool for me, but not essential to my life like it was for some kids at school. A girl once dropped hers in the toilet while I was in the washroom, and from her reaction, I thought someone had died. She completely lost her mind over it. If my phone was gone, it was gone. There were no incriminating photos on it, and my contact list had only four numbers in it, all pro-grammed by Kris. Her home, cell, and work numbers and the school's number. Kris had bought the phone for me when I'd first moved in and losing it looked like I didn't appreciate having it, which wasn't the case. If it was really lost, I'd need to pay for a new one.

I grabbed a snack and went to my room. The re-search I'd done on the circus, or side show, was the tip of the iceberg. I wanted to know more. I closed the cur-tains, which Kris had opened due to her annoying belief that sunlight belonged in a bedroom. I liked it dark and cocoon-like. Throwing my jacket onto a heap of clothes on the floor, I sat on my bed and leaned over to drag the laptop out from under it.

The cabinet card photos I'd found the previous night popped up first. I found a Pinterest page with hundreds of them, collected from flea markets and vin-tage stores. I scrolled farther down the page of imag-es, past Ella and Elvira and Ahmed, to one of Daniel dressed in a formal suit. The high collar of his dress shirt looked wrong with his hairy face. Like a dog in a costume. The effect was probably intentional. He stood unsmiling, staring into the camera. *The Rarest of Rare! Dog-Faced Boy Is a Genius!* I remembered Monsieur Duval onstage introducing Daniel, telling the crowd how he belonged on a Shakespearean stage with the finest actors of the world.

I searched until I found all of them. My breath caught in my throat when I found a cabinet card of a woman sitting on a chair. Her skirt was raised to expose four legs. She grinned sweetly. Her blond hair was bobbed, and she had a flower tucked behind her ear. *Mathilde the Four-Legged Woman*, the card read. I felt a tug at my heart and stared at her for a long time. This was the woman Frances had called Mama. It had to be.

A few photos down I found one labelled *Travelling Side Show c. 1921*. It was a group portrait of the performers. Everyone stood stiffly, their expressions sombre. Only Ahmed showed a hint of a smile. I looked closely at the grainy photograph, enlarging it on the screen. Standing beside Mathilde was a child in a lacy Victorian dress. It was Frances.

I zoomed in on her face. The scales of her skin were so perfectly shaped, they looked drawn on. She gazed into the camera with a confident tilt of her chin.

Of all the performers pictured, she and Mathilde were the only ones I hadn't seen at the warehouse circus.

I put the laptop back on the floor and reached for the ankh. Having barely slept last night, I was happy to slide under the covers now. Closing my eyes, I waited to slip back into Frances's world.

17

FROM MY SPOT AT THE PICNIC TABLE, I could see Gus running across the field. He was jumping like a puppy, trying to catch the dandelion fluffs that floated in the wind. I'd used to call them flower fairies when I was little. Mama would sit in a field with me, puff her cheeks, and blow them off their stems. But I was too old for that silliness now.

I was wearing my fancy white dress trimmed with eyelet lace. Papa had bought the lace off a peddler and gotten it made into a real and proper dress for me. It had a sash of pink satin that matched the one in my hair. Mama used to roll my hair in rags, but there was no one to do that now, so it hung long and loose over my shoulders. I looked like Esmerelda, my favourite paper doll. Well, except for the crackling lizard skin.

A chemist had once given Papa a cream for it. Some ointment he thought could cure it, but Papa had tossed it in the fire. I'd watched the tin turn black and warp as the flames licked it. "He's a fool," he'd said and crouched down beside me, letting a ringlet curl around his finger. "You will be a wealthy woman one day, Frances. Like your mama." He'd raised his eyes to find Mama standing behind me. "Your skin is your ticket to fame and fortune. People will always be intrigued by the things they cannot understand. Never be ashamed of who you are."

After Papa left, Mama found a stick and dragged the blackened tin out of the ashes. I watched her, curious. She grinned at me. "Men don't understand, do they?" she'd whispered. "What's the harm in trying?"

"Papa said —"

"I know what Papa said." The smile stayed on her lips, but her eyes hardened. "But Papa's perfect. No one stares at him like they do at us."

I'd never thought of that before. Papa was on stage, same as the rest of us, as the announcer. But there was nothing about him that made him a marvel. Mama let the tin cool, then pried off the lid. Whatever had been inside had run out, a hole burnt in the lid. Mama tossed it back onto the fire, frowning in disappointment.

"It's not your fault about your skin," she'd told me. "And Papa's right, you should never be ashamed of what you are. But this life is hard. It used to be different." Mama had travelled with shows ever since she was younger than me. She spoke of her past wistfully. "We'd stay in hotels, and the best theatres in the country wanted our show on their stages. There were thick velvet curtains and two floors of seats filled." She grinned at me, her eyes wide with longing. "You should have seen my gowns." She sighed. "The world's changing, Frances. We've got to change with it."

She rubbed her thumb on my cheek. A piece of dried-up skin flaked off. "I'm your mama. Maybe I didn't give birth to you, but I am. My job is to protect you. If it means leaving what we know to find a better life, I'll do it." Her face, usually so serene, lit up with ferocity. She looked at me hard with her blue eyes and then pulled me into a hug, pushing my head against her chest and clutching me to her.

The memory faded as performers buzzed past me now, getting ready for the show. The circus would be opening soon. A crowd had already gathered at the front gates, eager to flood inside. Papa's voice rang out, tempting them with what they'd find inside. For only a few cents, they would gain admission to Monsieur Duval's Circus of Marvels and Wonders. Thor stamped his feet at a couple of heads that poked under the canvas fence. "Off with you!" he bellowed menacingly. The boys took off, howling.

I tucked my paper dolls back into their metal box and wove my way through our sleeping quarters, a collection of tents and wagons we set up in a circle behind the main tent. From between the canvas screens, I got a view of the waiting crowd. The people in the line were a mixture of ages: lots of children with parents, men and women out for an afternoon, and a gang of boys. I gave a silent groan. I didn't like seeing boys in the audience. Some of them pointed and laughed, their tone cruel. They weren't here to be astounded. They just wanted to make fun, get their eyeful of Concetta and Shirley. They'd shrink back from Daniel when Papa told them how he'd lived like an animal in the forest before his transformation into a refined actor.

And then I took the stage as Alligator Girl. I'd walk out as a proper young lady while Papa regaled them with the story of how I was found in a swamp, eating mice for dinner. I had to bare my teeth at that point and snap at the audience menacingly, taunting them. They'd gasp, horrified. Papa would explain how he'd tamed me of my reptilian ways, and then I'd curtsy, sweet as pie. He said the only remnant from my swamp birth was my skin.

Papa would invite the crowd to come closer, to take a good look. They'd surge to the stage, jockeying for position. Mothers would hold their little ones back, clutching at them anxiously. Sometimes, seeing the way the mothers kept their children close, protecting them, made me miss Mama, and tears would spring to my eyes. But I'd blink them away. I wasn't allowed to cry onstage, no matter what.

"Frances, you shouldn't be there." Daniel, already dressed in his suit, caught me at my peeking spot. "They'll be opening the gates soon." For all of Papa's storytelling about what a beastly creature Daniel had been, he was the kindest and most gentle of men.

Reluctantly, I pulled myself away from the fence and followed him through the tent flap that led to the stage. The audience would come in through the main door and take their seats. Already, Ahmed, Shirley, and Ella and Elvira had taken their spots, waiting to be called onstage by Papa. Shirley's bulk took up so much space. I was squeezed into a corner, and I could feel beads of sweat popping out on my forehead.

The tight space was too much to bear. I felt a pang of envy for Gus and his freedom. He could spend the afternoon doing what he pleased, so long as his chores were done. Sure, Papa was hard on him, but was that anything compared to standing up onstage to be gawked at by strangers, or waiting backstage for an hour and listening to Shirley mutter profanities as the crowd streamed in? She was always in a foul mood.

I heard Papa working the crowd. We had the mummy to view now, too, for an extra penny. The mysteries and secrets Papa promised them were too enticing to walk away from. Through a small tear in the canvas, I peeked out at the crowd. The gates opened and people streamed forward, speaking excitedly, not sure where to go first.

I spotted a group of boys imitating Concetta, pulling their arms into their shirts and making lewd gestures with their mouths. They pretended to be Thor by stomping around like a monster. I furrowed my brow watching them. Thor spoke three languages, and he had a gift with horses. Concetta's voice rivalled any professional singer's. All the boys saw was the reason we were onstage. They knew nothing about us.

"What about Alligator Girl?" one of them asked. He stuck his tongue in and out quickly, like a snake, snapping at his friends as they got close. There was a chorus of disgusted groans. I turned away from the hole in the tent, my stomach churning. They thought I was repulsive!

I'd never thought of myself that way before. I was a performer, like Papa said.

How could I go onstage now knowing what they thought of me? I looked at the growing group of performers around me. Shirley plucked at the strings of her ukulele that was comically tiny against her massive bulk. Ahmed had joined us now and was stretching, one leg held up to his head. Ella and Elvira primped and preened in a hand-held mirror. But they all wore the same dull expression. Another town, another show. We'd stay here for days or weeks until the crowds stopped coming, then we'd move on to a new place. A raucous laugh made my stomach churn again. Those boys were in the tent. They were waiting for me like bloodthirsty jackals. I had to escape.

I bent down, inching my way toward the back of the tent. I had a few minutes before Papa took the stage and began the show. If I was going to go, I had to do it now.

So I did. I crawled under the tent wall, gulping down fresh air and my sudden, unplanned freedom. I took off, my leather shoes slippery on the hand-packed earth. I didn't wear stockings — Papa wanted everyone to see the lizard skin on my legs — so the soles of my feet grew sticky with sweat as I ran. I turned sideways and slid between wooden frames supporting the canvas fence and found myself in the great wide open. My heart pounded as I put more distance between myself and the circle of tents.

I spotted Gus standing at the top of the hill, one hand shielding his eyes from the sun. "What're you doing?" he called to me.

"What's it look like?"

"You're supposed to be onstage!"

I fixed him with a look. "I'm taking a break today."

"Does your Papa know?" His forehead creased with worry.

I didn't want to think about Papa or what he'd do when he called my name and I didn't step forward. Instead, I tapped him on the shoulder. "You're it!" I called and took off. I wasn't Alligator Girl anymore. I was Frances, playing tag with my friend in a sunny field. The walls of the circus weren't holding me captive today. I heard Gus behind me, his fingertips stretching out, almost brushing against my shoulder as I raced down the hill. I went so fast my legs spun under me with a will of their own. The shoes had no grip and I started to tumble.

I fell hard on my knees and then rolled in a somersault down the hill.

"Frances!" Gus yelped.

I landed on my back and stared up at the blue sky and the late-day sun. White fluffs filled the air, floating around us. *Maybe this is what heaven feels like.*

Gus stuck his face in mine. "Are you all right?" He scanned me for injuries. "Your dress."

I looked down. The front of my dress was covered in grass stains and dirt smudges. A torn piece of lace dangled from the hem. A sick feeling rose in my stomach. How would I hide that from Papa?

"Frances!" We both sat up. Papa's voice bellowed from the other side of the hill. "Frances!"

"He's looking for you!"

I didn't want to go back. I didn't want to face those boys and everyone else who'd paid money to see me. I grabbed Gus's arm, throwing him off balance. He landed beside me in the grass. "Lie down. Pretend you're asleep. Quick!" He did as he was told, slowing his breath so it matched the rhythm of mine. My eyelids wanted to open a crack, but I kept them pressed together. Papa's voice got closer, his yells more distressed. He crested the hill and caught sight of us. "Frances!" He shouted with relief. But it was short lived.

He shook my shoulders roughly and my eyes flew open.

He was still in his suit. His top hat blocked out the sun, casting shadow on me. "What are you doing?" Each word was punctuated with spittle that flew into my face. He turned to Gus, narrowing his eyes. "This is your doing," Papa sneered at him.

Gus pulled his knees to his chest and stared up at him, fearful.

"We were playing and we fell asleep," I mumbled. I didn't want Gus to get in trouble.

Papa glared at me. "There's a tent full of customers waiting to see Alligator Girl," he snapped. He made it sound as if I owed them something, these people who came to ogle. My eyes filled with tears, which he must have taken for guilt, because the anger drained from his face. He bent down and raised my chin to meet his eyes. "They come from far away to see you. They talk about you and word spreads. You are famous already. They will make you rich, Frances."

I gave a contrite nod of my head. From the corner of my eye, I could see Gus watching us.

"Never run off like that again, you understand? I was worried about you." He turned to Gus. "And you. I'll deal with you later."

"Don't blame Gus. It was my idea to play tag and to lie down and look at clouds. We fell asleep, is all."

Papa clenched his mouth and surveyed my stained and ripped dress. "Come. We have to get you cleaned up. I'll make up a story about you sneaking off to hunt mice in the field. Bare your teeth when I talk about it, or stick out your tongue. Understand?"

"But I wasn't hunting mice. I was playing."

Papa scoffed. "They haven't paid to see a normal girl onstage," he reminded me as he marched toward the tents. An overwhelming feeling of dread crept up on me as we got closer.

Papa sent me into the tent the same way I'd escaped. Ahmed was onstage now, entertaining the crowd with his contortionist routine. Shirley must have gone on first, because she wasn't waiting backstage anymore. The crowd oohed and aahed in the right places as Ahmed bent and twisted his body.

I stood in the shadows, collecting myself, trying to push away the nausea that crept up my throat. I'd done this a hundred times before, I reminded myself. Two shows a day since I was old enough to hold Papa's hand and waddle onstage.

But today felt different. Something had changed.

"Mothers, hold your children close! The Alligator Girl is a reptilian creature!" Papa called out in his ringmaster's voice, deep and round. "The missing link between our world and that of the swamp!"

I edged my way toward the stage. The group of raucous boys had taken their seats in the front row. Their wild-eyed, giddy smiles made me shrink back. Who was the real creature to fear? I wondered, watching them.

The crowd gasped as Papa's embellishment grew. "This young girl was raised by an alligator mother as one of her own. Taking pity on the creature, I wrestled her out of the vicious creature's nest. She snapped and clawed at me like a wild thing, but still I fought to bring her to civilization. You will see in a moment how the Alligator Girl has been tamed. But even now, she longs to return to that nest in the swamp, to live among the man-eating alligators with her reptilian mother!"

That was all lies, of course. Papa never talked about the woman who had given birth to me. But Mama had. She'd told me that a treasure like me wasn't meant for a regular family. Soon as I came into this world, the midwife had called Papa. It was pure luck that the circus had been in town. Mama said from the moment he laid eyes on me, he knew I was special. He'd brought me back to the circus, and he and Mama had raised me as their own.

Onstage, Papa gave a devilish grin and continued his story about me. "Be warned, she is wild! Part reptile, part human. Here is … Alligator Girl!" That was my cue to step forward, but my feet were frozen to their spot in the shadows. The crowd waited in suspense — even the boys had quieted down — but I couldn't move. Papa's back stiffened. He shot me a look from the stage.

"Go!" Gus hissed in my ear. He'd appeared beside me, and now he gave me a shove, and I ended up in front of the audience. Papa was at centre stage. I was meant to go to him so he could caress my head to prove how I'd been tamed. I could feel the audience's eyes on me. Papa called it "marvelling," but I thought of the boys and wondered if it was something else.

He stretched out his hand, beckoning me, but I couldn't do it. I froze again. His brow furrowed. "Perhaps she is timid today. Please, let's encourage her." The crowd clapped. The boys hollered. Papa gave me a warning glare.

I turned to look at Gus waiting offstage. Would he follow me if I ran?

"Eww, look at her skin," one of the boys snickered to his friend.

A flush rose up my neck. I felt naked and exposed.

"Frances," Papa's voice was stern. But something had shifted in me. I didn't want to be onstage. I lifted my head and met his eyes. With a small shake of my head, I stayed where I was. He pressed his lips together, colour rising in his cheeks. "Frances, don't be like that. These people have come to see you." I heard the catch in his voice. His cajoling was a cover for fear of what I might do.

No, they haven't. I looked into the crowd: at the mothers who hugged their children close, their lips stretched in revulsion, and the boys in the front who gawked.

Papa's eyes flashed with icy anger. A small spark of rebellion flared in me. Mama hadn't wanted this for me.

She'd been planning to save me, to leave the show and have a future.

"No."

Hearing the word echo in the stillness made my breath catch in my throat. I'd never openly defied him before. His face paled.

I turned on my heel and raced off the stage.

⚜

I woke up sweating. Images of the dream thudded in my brain: the laughing boys, Monsieur Duval's shock, Frances's thudding heart.

It took me a minute to collect myself. I was still tangled in Frances's world.

With a deep breath, I sat up and looked around. I was in my room. Safe. There were black smudges of eye makeup streaked across my pillow, and I'd kicked the covers off my bed. A clatter of dishes in the kitchen made me jump. A drawer slammed. I glanced at the clock. Kris was home.

I needed to get everything from the dream down on paper: the way Frances had felt onstage, the leering eyes of the boys, and the growing conflict between her and Monsieur Duval. Mr. Kurtis had told me to figure out what Frances wanted. Now I knew. She wanted out of the circus.

18

THE NEXT MORNING, I went straight to Mr. Kurtis's room. But when I got there the door was locked, and the lights were off. I'd been drawing for hours the night before and wanted to show him what I'd done. The story from my dreams was taking shape in the pages of my sketchbook.

"Isn't he usually here early?" It was the wannabe April. The same one who'd come early yesterday. Her dark hair was stuck up in a bun today, not styled in bouncy curls. Wearing sweats and a hoodie, she looked like she'd rolled out of bed and come right to school.

"Yeah. Usually," I muttered. "Maybe he had a meeting." From my experience, talking to girls like her backfired. She might be civil to me in private, or if we had to partner for a project, but as soon as someone she knew was around, I was forgotten.

She groaned. "I really needed to talk to him. I can't fail art."

I snorted. "How can you fail art? You just have to hand your work in."

"I owe him like ten assignments. My volleyball coach is benching me until I get my mark up." She bit her lip, but couldn't stop her chin from trembling. I stared, shocked to see her close to tears. "I'm falling behind in all my classes."

Wannabe April leaned against the wall. "I thought if I could catch up in one ..." Her voice trailed off.

I hated to admit it, especially after the way girls like her had treated me, but I felt myself softening a little. I knew how she felt. Before I could stop myself, I blurted out, "I might be able to help."

"Really?"

I nodded. "For a price." I wasn't a total sucker.

Wannabe April looked at me doubtfully. "How much?"

"Ten assignments, ten bucks each. They'll be done by tomorrow." It wouldn't get me a new phone, but it might be enough for a used one, or at least a down payment to Kris.

She weighed her options. "You have to make them look like my work."

"Obviously. I'll need your sketchbook and half the money now."

She balked at that. "Half? I'm not giving you anything until the work is done."

"Suit yourself," I said with a shrug.

Wannabe April let loose another frustrated groan. "Fine! I'll give you forty because that's all I have. And the work has to be done by tomorrow morning."

I held out my hand for the payment and her sketchbook. "Nice doing business with you, April."

"My name's not April," she said, giving me a weird look. "It's Jessica."

I shrugged. "You're all April to me," I muttered as she walked away.

Flipping through her book, I wondered if she'd taken art because she thought it would be an easy A, or because she had a crush on Mr. Kurtis. She hadn't put much effort into any of the first assignments, and she didn't have the right supplies, either. Her sketchbook was dollar-store quality, and I could tell by the thickness of her pencil strokes that she was using a standard HB instead of the 2B Mr. Kurtis wanted us to use. I felt a bit bad about asking for so much money. Maybe those were the best supplies she could afford.

There was one decent piece. The self-portrait we'd been assigned was surprisingly good, not because of her technique, but the idea behind it. Jessica was pulling a mask away from her face to reveal another face that was the exact same. *Not bad.* She might not be as vapid as her friends.

At lunch, I went to the library and worked on Jessica's assignments. The library at Henderson High had lots of open spaces and big tables meant for collaboration. I was more of a private study carrel girl myself. There was a table I'd discovered last year at the back, hidden in a corner behind the bookshelves. I'd gouged *This table is death* on the surface, which had worked surprisingly well at keeping people away.

Flipping through Jessica's sketchbook, I saw that she had completed the first few assignments of the term. But a month ago, just after the self-portrait, her work had basically stopped. She'd started a few pieces and lost interest. I used those beginnings as my inspiration, and by the time lunch was over, I had completed two of them. I might be able to make good money being a bad-artist imposter. Although, being authentically bad at something I was naturally good at was a lot harder than I'd thought.

19

"GOOD NIGHT," Kris called from the hallway. I hadn't told her about my money-making venture, but I'd spent all night in my room working on Jessica's sketches. Kris had talked to the phone company to find out how much a replacement phone would cost. It looked like I was going to have to draw a lot more bad art if I wanted a new one.

Max hadn't shown up for school, not that I'd expected him to. I wished I had a way to get a hold of him. I wondered if his dreams had changed, like mine had. Kris's cop friend hadn't found out anything about Monsieur Duval. With no birthdate or address to go on, it had been a long shot. The warehouse was owned by a numbered company, and the occupant was listed as vacant, so the Circus of Marvels and Wonders had been there illegally, which didn't surprise me. I was no further ahead in figuring out who Monsieur Duval was or how he'd found me.

The only thing that was shedding light on the present were my dreams of the past. As I tossed Jessica's sketchbook to the floor and closed my eyes, I could almost feel Monsieur Duval on the other side, waiting for me.

I wanted to run and run as far away as I could and leave the tent with the laughing boys. I turned once to see if Papa was coming after me and ran smack into Shirley. Shirley had come to us from the south and had an accent that was as round and warm as she pretended to be onstage. Her routine was a storytelling act with a bit of singing accompanied by her ukulele. She made jokes about her own weight, inviting the crowd to laugh at her. But offstage she had mean eyes and made nasty comments about the other performers behind their backs. She didn't like Papa, and I don't think he liked her.

"What are you doing running around at showtime? Shouldn't you be onstage, girl?" Shirley barked at me.

Tears sprang to my eyes thinking of the way I'd left Papa alone onstage. But the thought of those hungry eyes ravaging my skin was too much. I balled my hands into fists. *I'll never go onstage again*, I swore.

Shirley grabbed my elbow. "Get yourself in my tent before someone sees you. Jesus almighty, girl." She hustled me into her tent and collapsed onto some propped-up pillows, her breathing laboured. Her costume gave the audience a good look at the fat that pooled around her ankles. She had legs as big as tree trunks and a stomach that spilled around her middle onto the chair she sat on.

"So? Where were you goin'?"

I buttoned my lip. Even if I'd had a plan, I'd have been hesitant to tell her a thing.

"I know where," she said, fanning herself. "Got it in your mind you're too good for this circus, ain't that right? I told Philippe treating you so good was gonna give you a big head."

I watched her carefully. She shifted her weight and a spoiled milk smell rose up. Unwashed flesh. I ducked my head away from it.

"Something you should understand. What kind of future you think a girl like you is gonna have? You think you're gonna have babies with a face like that?" She pointed her fan at my face. "What man would want you in bed with him? Riskin' his babies will turn out same as you?"

My face prickled with humiliation.

"I'm not trying to hurt you, but these're the facts of life for us. We gotta get while the getting's good, girl. If those lookie-loos wanna pay to laugh and point and snicker at us, well, I say let 'em. Better'n walkin' down the street and lettin' people do it for free."

"But what if — what if I don't want to do it?"

She squinted at me and leaned forward. I worried she'd tumble to the ground. "And what else would you be doin'? Huh? No one's gonna take care of a girl like you. You count yourself among the lucky ones. You got that pretty blond hair and them fancy dresses." She ran her eyes over me with undisguised jealousy. "Your life ain't so bad. You're just uppity like Mathilde."

I glared at her.

"Oh-ho-ho. Look at you with those angry eyes. You *are* just the same as her."

"You don't know what you're talking about."

Shirley snorted. "Miss High 'n' Mighty." She fixed me with a cold stare. "I heard 'em, Mathilde and Philippe, arguing the night she died. She wanted to leave and take you with her. Philippe said no, but she left anyway, didn't she? She was too used to getting her way."

"Mama —"

"She weren't your mama, girl. That's one more dream you were living. Your mama was some whore that screamed at the sight of you. You probably would've been drowned if the midwife hadn't known 'bout Monsieur Duval. Soon as he saw you, he had dollar signs dancing in his eyes."

I balled up my fists, and I would have taken a swing at her if I'd thought it would do any good. "Shut your mouth!" I shouted, stomping my foot. "I hate you!"

Shirley hooted with laughter, which made me angrier. "I don't give a rat's fanny what you think about me, girl."

"You're a fat ugly cow!"

Shirley's eyes glinted like the blade of a chisel. Her voice got quiet and deep. "You think that's the worst anyone's said to me? Take a look in the mirror, girl. We're all ugly cows. Every one of us. All's we got is each other. No one's gonna save us from this life. You think about that. What'd you do without this circus? Huh? Count your lucky stars Monsieur Philippe Duval came along when he did. This circus is all we got. *Each other* is all we got. Ain't no one begging to be let into this place. We're here because we don't have other choices."

"Gus does."

"What's that?" She narrowed her eyes at me.

"Gus chose to stay with us."

She snorted. "He's a fool. What's gonna happen soon as he's old enough to fend for himself? He's gonna find some pretty girl in town and leave your lizard-skin ass behind."

"He wouldn't do that."

"Oh, no?" she raised a skeptical eyebrow, and a new surge of hate flowed from me.

"There you are!" Papa burst through the flap in Shirley's tent. I'd thought he'd be angry, but it was concern that lined his face.

"Papa!" I cried and flew at him, wrapping my arms around his chest.

He held me out at arm's length. "What happened?" His voice was sharp. He would not be fooled by theatrics.

All that had been swirling in my head suddenly evaporated. I bowed my head, ashamed. Papa put his finger under my chin and tilted my face up to his. "You didn't need to run." He crouched down. Through the flap of the tent, I caught a glimpse of Gus hovering outside.

"I didn't want them looking at me," I whispered to him. As quiet as my voice was, Shirley heard and harrumphed.

"I miss Mama." My voice was thick with tears. I wondered how he heard me at all.

He stroked my hair. "I know." I clung to him tighter. When Papa spoke, I knew he was close to crying, too. "Say thank you to Shirley for looking after you," he instructed me.

I refused at first, sullenly staring at the floor. Papa's grip tightened. "Thank you," I whispered. As we left, I turned and stuck my tongue out at her.

"You've got him to thank for saving you today," Papa said, nodding at Gus as we left Shirley's tent. Gus had found a stick, and was whittling it, as if unconcerned about the events of the afternoon. But there was something different in the way he held his head — a new-found confidence. "After you ran, he started moaning offstage as if he'd been attacked, even clawed up his own face to make it believable." Gus turned his face to me and showed off some bloody scratches across his cheek. "He got onstage and played out a scene that had me hanging on every word. Quite an actor you are, Gus. We might have to put that to good effect some other time."

Gus blushed at the words. Jealousy bit at me. It was my own fault for taking off, but I'd never heard Papa praise another child before.

"You might not be such a waste after all," Papa said to him. "Frances, we need to get that dress cleaned and repaired." My breath caught in my throat. Hadn't he heard anything I'd said? I didn't want to go back on-stage. But Shirley's warnings rang in my ears. If I didn't perform, what would happen to me?

"I have to get back to the show," he said. From where we were, we heard applause and laughter filling the air. "Yuri is almost finished." He nodded at Gus. "Keep her safe." I felt Gus's eyes on me as I walked across the yard to the wagon I shared with Papa.

"Frances," Gus said, jogging to catch up with me. "Why are you upset?"

I shouldered him away. He wouldn't understand. He wasn't a marvel. He'd never know what it was like to be gawked at.

When the afternoon show had finally finished and the spectators were gone, I made my way to Abeline's tent. Now forgotten on the fringes of the circus, Abeline had once been a performer. She'd been one of the first stars of the side show circuit. Billed as the Four-Legged Woman, she had had a twin who had never fully formed. Her extra legs stuck out of her hunched back. They'd atrophied over time, and now they flopped around like dead fish. Most of the time she kept them wrapped under a strip of fabric, which made her hunched back even more pronounced. I'd heard other performers talk of the crowds she'd drawn. One of her posters still hung in Papa's wagon.

But age isn't friendly to circus acts, and as she got older, people grew less interested in seeing her. They wanted someone young and attractive. And then Mama came along. She'd had a twin, too. Her second pair of legs hung down between her own — a true four-legged woman. Mama was angelic, with round apple cheeks and blue eyes. When she wore her long skirts, no one would have guessed about the extra legs. She waddled, of course, making room for the legs, but she looked normal. The audience would gasp when she lifted her skirts onstage to reveal the dangling, useless limbs hiding under her dress. Mama would titter and giggle modestly, but she'd told me that when she stepped onstage, she turned off inside. And if you'd looked at her eyes, you could tell that wasn't Mama in there. She was going about the motions, giving the people what they wanted. It was when we were alone that she came alive. When we cuddled together on her big straw mattress, Papa would regale us with stories, legends passed down from his Cree grandmother, and Mama would hold me tight, stroking my hair.

I was so distracted thinking about Mama that I almost walked past Abeline's tent. "Hey there, girl," she called out. A fire crackled and a pot of boiling water bubbled over it.

I was shy around Abeline. She stuck to herself, choosing to eat meals alone even though she cooked for the rest of us. She was missing most of her teeth, so I had to listen carefully to understand her. "Your pa told me you were coming by." She waved for me to sit down on an upside-down crate. I handed her the dress, and she held it up, inspecting it. She shook her head at the torn lace.

She rubbed white paste on the grass and mud stains. Her gnarled fingers moved slowly. I watched impatiently, unsure if I was allowed to leave.

"How old are you now?"

"Ten," I answered.

A toothless grin spread across her face. "Mathilde was that age when she joined the circus. I was old news soon as your papa found her. A beauty, she was. I knew she'd be a star soon as I saw her. Your pa did, too." She'd told me this story lots of times, but I nodded and let her tell me again.

She groaned as she rose to put the dress into the boiling pot of water. "Getting old's a terrible thing, Frances," she muttered. Taking in her slow feet and hunched back, I didn't doubt it. "Enjoy your youth."

She stirred the dress around with a stick. I looked away. She reminded me of a witch at a cauldron. She took out the sopping dress and waited for it to cool.

"Anyone ever tell you what happened to your mama?"

I shook my head. They didn't need to. I'd been with her, hiding in the shadows, although no one knew that. I remembered all too well what had happened that night. How she'd woken me while the rest of the circus slept and dug out our bags from under the bed, already packed, whispering that she'd heard about a doctor in the next town who could help fix my skin.

"Some men got hold of her. Wanted to see what was under those skirts of hers."

We'd been in the woods, following a trail that led to town, keeping out of sight. A camp of woodcutters heard us and stood with rifles aimed our way. "They think we're thieves," Mama had said to me. "Stay here. Keep out of sight." She crouched on the ground with me. There was no way around them unless we went back to the circus.

"Who's there?" they called, their voices slurred with drink.

"Evening, gentlemen," Mama had said, rising.

Abeline continued, "She never had to look after herself before. Always had all of us around her. Don't know what made that girl think she could go off on her own like that."

A quick stab of guilt pierced my heart. For me. She'd left for me.

"One of the men must have recognized her. Maybe from the show." Abeline's attention drifted off, her eyes glazing over. "Or maybe seeing a pretty young thing in the woods was all it took. Those men went after her."

I'd heard her cry out as they grabbed her. I was too scared to do anything, worried they'd get me, too. The men shouted like it was a sport, egging each other on. I knew it was bad. Her cries were filled with fear. I tried to block them out. I didn't know what to do. She'd said to wait, but how could I? They were hurting her! Finally, I'd stood. I had to get Papa. I looked back once and saw Mama pinned to the ground, her skirts lifted. All four legs exposed and her drawers off.

"Did things to your Mama. Ruined her."

Branches had scratched my face and torn at my clothes as I raced back to the circus. I had to get Papa. Yuri saw me first. His white face glowed in the dark. Breath cut my throat in heaving rasps. "Mama," I gasped. "Men."

I cried and pointed out the path. He ran to get Papa. I went to hide in the wagon. I was too terrified to do anything else. I curled in a ball in the corner, shivering with fear and waiting for Mama to come back to me.

"Philippe got the others and they went looking for her. Searched till they found her body in the woods." Abeline looked at me. I knew the colour had drained from my face. Mama's agonized screams echoed in my head. "I ain't telling you the story to hurt you," Abeline said. "I'm telling you so you remember who's your family. All's we got in this life is each other. Ain't no one else looking out for us. And when we pass, it'll be these folks here who'll remember us for who we really are."

She held up my dress. The stains were gone. "Be as good as new when I'm done with it. Come back tomorrow, and it'll be ready for you."

I stood to go.

"How about a thank you?" she asked.

I looked at the wizened old hag. I didn't believe her when she said she hadn't told me the story to hurt me. Something harsh ran in her blood, same as Shirley. Maybe years of standing on a stage and being gawked at did that to a person. I shook my head, turned, and walked to Papa's wagon, with Mama's screams still ringing in my head.

When I woke up, Frances's pain clung to me. She was starting to realize what I'd known for a long time.

The world isn't kind to people like us.

I T WAS GETTING HARDER AND HARDER to leave Frances's
world behind. I thought about her as I walked to
school. And as soon as I arrived, I went to Mr. Kurtis's
room so I could keep working on my drawings of last
night's dream.

"Morning," Mr. Kurtis said.

"Is it okay if I work in here?" I asked.

He looked up from his computer. "Yeah, of course.
Still working on that graphic novel?"

I hadn't realized that that was what I was creating,
but now that Mr. Kurtis pointed it out, I saw he was right.
I'd put the scenes in frames, using different perspectives,
and there was a narrative, just like in *Persepolis*, the book
we were studying in English.

I nodded and pulled my sketchbook out of my bag,
careful to keep Jessica's hidden. Her sketches were finished. Now I needed to find a way to get them to her.

Flipping my sketchbook open to the page I'd been working on this morning, I tilted my head to examine the close-up sketch of Abeline's withered face. Without teeth, her lips needed to pucker more. I was so engrossed in drawing that I didn't hear anyone come into the room until a chair scraped against the floor beside me. From the corner of my eye, I saw Max.

"I have a surprise for you," he said.

"What?" I asked without looking at him.

"I found it," Max said. He held out my phone.

I stared at it incredulously. "Where? How?"

He put it on the desk in front of me. "I went back to the warehouse and looked around."

I shook my head, not sure what to make of him. "Thanks," I said. I picked it up and pressed the power button, but it was dead. "How'd you get back in there?"

"I found a broken window in the basement." He leaned over my shoulder to see what I was drawing. "Another dream?"

"Yeah," I said and closed the cover on my sketch-book. For some reason, I wanted to keep Frances's world private. The deeper I got into it, the more I felt like her story was meant for me and no one else. The dream last night about her mama's death had left me surprisingly sad. I wasn't just watching the events; I was part of them. Frances's pain had become my pain.

And there was something else. Her pain felt familiar. Had I known what losing a parent felt like?

"Kris is cool. Letting me stay the other night," His voice drifted off. "You're lucky."

I snorted at the word *lucky*. If he knew more about my past, he'd know I'd been anything but lucky.

Mr. Kurtis looked up from his computer and noticed

Max was in the room. Mr. Kurtis let me hang out here because I spent the time sketching. Max was just sitting here.

"Are you here to catch up on your assignments?" Mr. Kurtis asked.

At the mention of schoolwork, Max stood up. "I was just leaving." To me, he said more quietly, "See you around, *Frances.*"

My head snapped up at the name.

Max smirked at my reaction as he left the room. His surprise visit and the way he'd called me Frances zapped my concentration. For the next twenty minutes, I did nothing but stare at the page in front of me.

Jessica didn't show up at the art room before the first bell. Which made sense — she didn't want Mr. Kurtis to catch her paying for assignments. I kept my eyes open for her as I went to bio. I'd been looking forward to giving her the sketchbook, and not just for the money. I'd left a surprise in her book. A freebie. It was the self-portrait of Jessica wearing a mask under a mask. I'd redrawn the whole thing, and it was impressive, if I did say so myself.

My run-in with the original April when I was a kid had turned me off trying to make friends. It wasn't worth the risk of being shot down. But looking at Jessica's self-portrait had made me wonder if I wasn't the only one hiding something. My armour ensured that the people I didn't want to be friends with stayed away, but it also pushed away anyone with potential. Except for Max. I thought back to the first day I'd met him, when he'd complimented my makeup. I had my phone back, thanks to him. Under the street kid toughness, there was something sweet, too.

The hall was clearing for first period when I saw Jessica dart into the girls' washroom. That was as good a place as any to give her back her sketchbook. Two Grade 9s saw me and scurried away. "Jessica?" I called when I got inside. My voice echoed off the tile walls.

"What?"

"I finished the sketches."

"So just leave them."

"I will. After you pay me."

There was no toilet flush before she came out of the stall. The door banged shut behind her. Smudges of mascara ringed her eyes and her nose was puffy and red. She looked past me to the mirror. "Oh god!" she moaned when she saw her reflection.

I kept my expression steely and held out the book. "It's sixty dollars."

She shot me a dirty look and yanked a paper towel from the dispenser. "All I have is a twenty." She turned on the cold water, wet the paper, and dabbed at her face.

"Then all you have are two more sketches." I opened the cover and was about to rip my other drawings out when she held up her hands.

"Okay, okay. Gawd. How about a little sympathy? It's been a crappy day, and it's only going to get worse."

I didn't want to care, but the words "How come?" slipped out, anyway.

"You wouldn't understand."

I snorted. "Try me."

The intense look I gave her must have worked. After living in foster homes and dealing with Foster Mom #2's

Boyfriend #3, there wasn't anything she could say that would surprise me.

"I told someone a secret, and now I wish I hadn't."

I knew about secrets. "Are they going to tell it?"

She nodded. "Probably."

"Is it bad?"

Jessica nodded again, slowly. "My friends are going to hate me."

"Would you hate them if it were the other way around?"

She didn't answer right away as she thought about the question. "I don't think so. I hope not." Jessica put both hands on the sink and stared at herself in the mirror. Hard. She took a deep breath, but the exhalation turned into a whimper. "Oh god. I can't go back to class. Not like this. I'm a mess."

"Here." I reached into my bag and pulled out my make-up pouch. I put it on the sink next to her. "There's some eyeliner and mascara ..." I trailed off, feeling ridiculous.

It was one of those moments that could have gone either way. I wouldn't have been surprised if she'd turned her nose up at the thought of sharing makeup with me, a goth girl. But she didn't. She pulled the bag closer and dug through until she found what she needed.

And then she got to work. It takes a lot of concentration to layer on makeup. It's like drawing on a moving canvas. I stood to the side and watched as she came back to life. When she was done, she put everything back into the makeup bag and zipped it shut. "Better?" she asked.

I nodded. I handed her the sketchbook, open to the redrawn self-portrait. "Pay me when you can." I had my phone back, thanks to Max. The money didn't matter as much anymore.

Her mouth hung open when she saw the drawing. "Frankie," she said, shocked, "it's amazing."

Some people were good with compliments. I wasn't one of them. "Good luck with your *friends*," I said and left the washroom. I'd been right about one thing. I wasn't the only one with something to hide. But I'd been wrong to deem Jessica a wannabe April. She was nothing like those girls.

21

"TA-DAH!" I held up my fully charged phone for Kris to see when she got home. She had a paper bag with her, and pulled two bottles of wine out of it.

"Is that *your* phone?" she asked.

"Max went back to the warehouse and found it. Lucky, huh?" Once it was charged, the first thing I'd checked was the video of the show, but there was no file. It was like I'd never pressed record. Had someone deleted it, or had it gotten erased by accident when I fell?

Kris's eyebrows drew together suspiciously. "Very lucky." She took the phone from me and inspected it. "Do you think Max might have had it the whole time?"

"I don't know. I can't figure that kid out. He seems so helpless sometimes, but he told me he basically lives on the streets."

"Did you ever get his last name?"

I shook my head. "In other news, I got a sixty percent on a bio quiz."

Kris whistled, impressed. "I'm glad one of us had a good day." She sighed and pulled the corkscrew out of the drawer.

Working as a child trauma counsellor, Kris had bad days that were far worse than other people's.

"Were you in court?"

She shook her head. The cork came out with a small pop. "It's that same case. Child trafficking. It'll be on the news." I could read on her face that the outcome hadn't been positive.

"Sorry," I murmured.

"Yeah, me, too." She poured herself a glass and went to the freezer to pull something out for us to eat.

For once, as I lay down, it wasn't Monsieur Duval, Frances, or Gus that I was thinking about; it was Jessica. Kris was always encouraging me to give people a chance, and today I had. Kris would call this progress.

When I was younger, I used to dream about my parents finding me. They'd scoop me up, crying and apologizing for having been gone so long. They'd have a logical reason for it, something out of their control, like an alien abduction or a spy mission. Memories of my happy childhood would flood back to me. I'd forgive them, and life would go on.

Now that I was older, those ideas were impossible and childish. I knew my parents weren't coming back for me. I'd stopped letting myself daydream about a joyful reunion. I'd stopped letting myself daydream at all. But tonight, for just a minute, I imagined what it would be like if the next morning at school, I walked past Jessica and she said hello.

I'd wave back, cool but friendly.

"See you in art class," she'd call, and laugh because it was sort of an inside joke.

Her friends would wonder what was going on, and as I walked away, I'd hear her say, "She's actually really cool. You should give her a chance."

Tears welled in my eyes. Imagining having a friend only made me feel lonelier, because it would probably never happen. I wiped the tears away and closed my eyes. I shut out thoughts of Jessica and concentrated on Frances. I needed to know what happened next.

Papa hadn't tucked me in for a long time. When I was smaller, he used to sit in the chair beside my cot and read me stories from an illustrated book of fairy tales by the Brothers Grimm. I loved the one about the ugly duckling the best. As I'd gotten older, it was Mama who'd sit with me until I fell asleep. And then, after she'd died, there had been no one.

But tonight, Papa was here.

I'd gone onstage today. There'd been a small crowd and no boys to mock me. Papa had rewarded me with a new pair of boots. They sat beside me on the pillow. I could smell the stiff leather and see the pearl buttons glistening in the lantern light. And something else.

"Here," Papa said, handing me a box. It was a perfect cube with gold curlicues embossed on the lid. "This is an extra special surprise."

"What is it?" I asked.

"Open it." His eyes danced in the lantern light.

I lifted the lid. Inside was a necklace.

"It's called an ankh," Papa said. "Mr. Hussein tells me it's magical." He drew out the word *magical* like he did with certain words onstage. It quivered in the air between us. I gave a wide berth to the mummy and to Mr. Hussein, who rarely left its side. The strange Egyptian man spoke in stilted English, but I thought he understood more than he let on. He watched us as if he knew our secrets. He didn't eat with us, preferring to stay in the mummy's tent.

I inspected the ankh necklace. It didn't look magical. It looked ugly. Heavy, with a pointy bottom and a chunky chain. I would have preferred sparkly costume jewellery like the kind Tabitha had.

"What makes it magical?" I asked.

Papa might have seen my look of disappointment, but he didn't let me dwell on it. He took the necklace out of the box and placed it over my head. I could tell by his smile that a story was coming.

"It captures souls," he said mysteriously.

Well, that was a little more interesting. We weren't churchgoers. It wasn't just all the moving around that kept us away from the ministers and priests. Papa said nothing good ever came from a man in a black robe.

"Could it capture Mama's soul?" I asked.

He smiled sadly. A lock of dark hair escaped the pomade he used to keep it slicked back. "Mama is always with us," he said. I fingered the strange pendant. The metal was blackened and in need of a good clean.

"We'll be moving soon," he told me. The troupe had been in this town for weeks, longer than we usually stayed anywhere. There had been set-up time, then rehearsals, and then the usual week of shows, but the weather had been good, and people had kept coming, so we'd been in no rush to move on. It had been a relief to stay put.

"Where will we go next?"

"Anywhere we want."

I tilted my head at Papa, sure he was joking. "Across the ocean?" I tested. "Europe?" Yuri was in charge of my schooling, and we'd been studying geography. I'd snuck the atlas away and kept it under my bed to show Gus. He hadn't believed the world was so big.

"We could even go to Egypt," Papa mused. "To see the Sphinx."

"That's where the mummy came from," I added.

The mummy had caused a stir in every town we'd gone to. The theatrics of its arrival had been forgotten now that it was just another part of our show. It was housed in its own tent, and people had to pay extra to see it. Bits of linen still clung to the torso, but its face was exposed, shrunken and black with age. It looked like a decrepit doll. There was another tent with other curiosities: horse fetuses trapped in jars and skeletons Papa had purchased from gravediggers and adjusted so they became two-headed humans. There was a mermaid, which was really a monkey's head attached to the body of a fish. Real or not, it didn't matter to the ticket buyers. As soon as Papa started his whispered story of a fierce, bloodthirsty mermaid he'd caught in the depths of the Indian Ocean, people stared at it wide eyed, eager to believe.

Papa had invented a story about the mummy being the body of a cursed Pharaoh. He warned audiences that only those who were pure of heart could escape the curse that haunted it. People lined up for hours to walk past it. The anxiety of the patrons who doubted themselves was obvious. Some fled at the last minute, bolting from the line with excuses, to the glee of neighbours.

"Yes, we could go to Egypt," Papa said, indulging me. He had a faraway smile. "Mathilde wanted to see the world," he murmured.

I snuggled into my quilt, enjoying our closeness. "I miss her."

"Me, too," he sighed, a hand absently stroking my cheek.

Papa began humming the song that Mama had used to sing. I was drifting off, her song in my head, when Papa stood to go.

"Papa?" I called into the growing darkness. "Tell me a secret." It had been a game we'd played when I was little. He'd whisper something silly to make me giggle. But tonight, when he spoke, there wasn't a trace of a smile on his face.

"We will all live forever. No one will be able to hurt us again."

He turned down the flame in my lantern, and I was left in the dark with that delicious thought.

22

I WAS AT THE TABLE, sketching my dream from the night before. Monsieur Duval's parting words lingered in my head. *We will all live forever.* I carefully outlined the ankh that he had given Frances. It was no coincidence that it looked the same as mine. What if it didn't just *look* the same — what if it *was* the same pendant? Could that be why Frances's dreams were coming to me so clearly?

When Kris walked into the kitchen, I opened my mouth to tell her my theory, then changed my mind.

She looked terrible. There were dark circles under her eyes, and her skin was pale. The nearly empty wine bottle on the counter might have had something to do with it. She didn't drink a lot, so whatever had happened yesterday at work had left a mark on her. "You should call in sick," I told her.

"I can't," she said with a resigned sigh. "Today might be better. It's just some of these kids —" she broke off, and I knew why. She'd literally brought her work home with her when she'd taken me in. My case might have been unusual, but I was just one of many kids mixed up in a system that she couldn't change. "They don't deserve what happens to them. No one does. And if one more person tries to make me feel better by saying kids are resilient, I'm going to throat-punch them."

"Whoa!" I looked up at her, shocked. I didn't get to see Feisty Kris very often, but when I did, I liked it.

"Being resilient doesn't mean you're going to be okay. It just means you don't give up."

"Isn't that kind of the same thing?"

"No. You still have to live with what happened." She had a point.

"Then stop being so good at your job, and you'll stop getting all the toughest cases," I suggested.

"Then they'd have no one." She gave me a sad smile. "More about the circus?" she asked, leaning over to look at my drawing.

"Technically, it's a side show," I corrected her, looking at the sketch with a critical eye. "The dreams feel so real."

As soon as I'd woken up, I'd started putting the images on paper. Sometimes they came too fast, and I couldn't keep up. Kris flipped back through pages and pages to the beginning of my drawings. "Every night is a continuation of the same story? And you're sure you're asleep? You're not just imagining it?"

I nodded. "Weird, huh?"

"I've heard of something similar happening under hypnosis. Repressed memories can surface that way." She frowned, "But you're asleep."

"And these aren't my memories. They belong to Frances. I see everything from her perspective."

Kris examined the drawings again. She looked a long time at the ones in which Frances witnessed Mathilde's death. I hadn't held back on those. Within my dream, Frances's memory had been vivid. Kris gave me a long, contemplative look. I knew what was going to come out of her mouth.

"These are really violent, Frankie. Intense. A psychologist could —"

I crossed my arms over my chest and shook my head. "No. I don't want to talk to anyone."

"These dreams, or whatever they are, aren't normal dreams." She pointed to one of the frames depicting Mathilde's attack. "All of this means something. It might explain what happened to you as a child."

The thought of explaining my life to a stranger was too daunting. My medical history, the Child and Family Services calls, Foster Mom #2's Boyfriend #3, and now this: a past life that was haunting my dreams. A shrink would have me committed to a psych ward in a heartbeat.

Was that what Kris wanted?

The little voice of doubt that never really left me spoke up. I looked at the almost empty wine bottle, the circles under her eyes, and the pleading expression on her face. She'd worked with me for seven years, even letting me move in with her. Maybe I'd worn her out. What if she wanted to use my dreams as a reason to get rid of me?

"You're worried about something," she guessed. "What is it?"

A lump grew in my throat. Kris reached for my hand and squeezed it, but I couldn't look at her.

"Frankie?"

It was still so hard to talk about things. To be vulnerable. The worry that Kris would abandon me was always my first thought.

I slid my hand out from under hers and tucked it under my arm. But Kris knew me well after all this time. It was hard to fool her.

"I chose you, Frankie. I'm here for the long haul. There's nothing you can do that's going to push me away. If you're not ready to talk to someone, I understand. I won't push it."

I gave her the side-eye, loving and hating that she knew me so well.

She put her hands on my shoulders, forcing me to look at her. "You can trust me, Frankie. I promise."

I took a deep breath. She'd said those words to me before.

The night I'd been found in the alley, one of the cops had shone a flashlight in my face and turned to his partner. "Look at her skin," he'd said. He'd grabbed my arm and pulled up the sleeve of my shirt, inspecting me. He'd lifted the front of my shirt and done the same to my stomach. I'd tried to twist away, but he'd held on tighter. "Are those scars?" he asked his partner.

They tried coaxing me out of the alley, offering me food and blankets, but I'd refused. I didn't know where I was or who I was; I couldn't answer their questions. How had I gotten there? Where were my parents? What was my name? My mind had been a blank, and that was the scariest thing of all.

When Kris arrived, she'd crouched down to sit on the cold, filthy pavement and told the cops to back off. They were scaring me.

"There's something wrong with her," the cop had said to her. "Check out her skin."

Kris had ignored him. I'd refused to look at her. Exhausted, cold, and hungry, I'd tucked my knees to my forehead and sat there sobbing. She must have sat with me for hours until the promise of food convinced me to go with her. We'd stood up, and she'd offered me her hand. Instinctively, I'd taken it.

"What is it?" Kris asked now.

"I was thinking about the night I was found. You told me then I could trust you."

She nodded, guilt clouding her eyes.

"I believed you."

My words hung between us. It wasn't the first time this had come up. Kris didn't make excuses. Guilt about what had happened to me was her cross to bear. She'd pulled me out of the alley with promises of protection, and instead I'd been wronged. Hurt by the system she worked in.

I could have blamed her, thrown her promises back in her face. But Kris was the only constant in my life since I'd been found. What I felt for her was more than love; it was deeper and more complicated. There was no easy description for our relationship. Maybe that was how all parent-child relationships were.

Even Monsieur Duval and Frances's, I realized.

I felt Kris's eyes on me. Icy-blue and honest. "I wasn't even supposed to be working that night. I was on over-time. I took the shift at the last minute because some-one had called in sick."

And from that fortuitous night onward, our lives had been intertwined. Through every crappy thing that had happened, Kris had been there for me. At my most anguished, I'd refused to see her, lashing out at the one person I knew I could hurt.

"We were meant to find each other. Me and you." She smiled at me. The little voice that wanted to ruin things was silenced.

23

THE FLAG AT THE ENTRANCE TO SCHOOL snapped in the wind. It had turned wintry overnight, and kids raced inside to escape the chill. Hard pellets of frozen rain spat down on me, and I hunched under my jacket, worried that my makeup would be ruined. I'd decided to wear the ankh pendant today, so I'd done my eyes Cleopatra-style: thick winged eyeliner with curls at the corners.

"Hey!"

I heard the voice, but didn't think it was directed at me until I heard it again. I turned. Jessica was there, holding the door for me. I stepped through, and she followed, matching my pace. "Here," she said, digging into her purse. "I have the rest of your money." It was rolled tightly, but a thick enough wad of bills that I trusted it was all there. She didn't let go of it when she passed it to me. Her voice dropped to a whisper. "I also wanted to tell you …" I leaned closer to hear, but when I did, her

forehead wrinkled. She wasn't looking at me anymore —
she was staring at my cheek. "You've got —" she broke
off, trying to figure it out. "What is that?"

My hands flew to my face. The spitting snow *had*
dampened my makeup! A few scales curled and peeled
under my fingertips. "Nothing," I said quickly and
ducked so my hair fell over my cheeks. I needed to get
to a washroom to see how bad it was.

I race walked through the foyer, shoulder-slamming
into someone in my rush to escape the crowd. As soon
as I got into the washroom, I went directly into a stall
and used my phone camera to inspect the damage. The
rain and the wind and the collar of my jacket had done
a number on my foundation. In lots of places, the makeup had rubbed away, and my dry, scaly skin was visible.

I needed a mirror like the one over the sink to re-
apply, and there was no way I was leaving the stall when
girls were still coming in and out before class.

"Frankie?" Jessica called. "Are you in here?"

What was she doing here?

I stayed silent, but a moment later a pair of brown
boots stopped outside my stall door. "I know it's you in
there. Your shoes are kind of obvious."

"What do you want?"

"There's no one else in here," she said. "You can
come out."

It was the last thing I wanted to do.

"I already saw, anyway. You've got like, eczema, or
something. It's not a big deal."

Eczema would have been a blessing compared to
lamellar ichthyosis. Obviously, she hadn't gotten a really good look at what was going on under the makeup.
But staying in the stall wasn't an option for much longer,

either. At least if Jessica was here, she could block the door while I fixed my makeup.

Slowly, I opened the metal latch. I could feel her watching me as I went to the sink. "It's not eczema," I told her. "It's something else that I don't want to talk about."

"I wasn't asking." But she did stand at the door, and when someone tried to come in, she told them to come back in five minutes. It was a very un-April thing to do.

I slathered on another thicker layer of foundation and avoided looking at Jessica.

"How long have you been goth?" she asked.

"Since Grade Seven."

She smirked. "I went through an emo stage when I was twelve. It was so stupid. I didn't even know what it meant. I just wanted to be different, you know? I wasn't moody enough to pull it off," she said with a self-deprecating laugh. "You're full on, though." She meant my hair, clothes, and makeup.

"I'd wear this makeup even if I wasn't goth. I don't like people looking at my skin."

Jessica nodded. "We all have things we don't like about ourselves," she said. But when I glanced at her in the mirror, I wondered what hers could possibly be. She didn't have one zit, one scar, or even a freckle. Her skin was a perfect olive-brown.

"This is different," I said quietly. "There's nothing I can do about it. It's a genetic condition. My skin peels constantly. It looks like I have scales."

Jessica frowned, digesting the information. "Do your parents have it, too?"

"I don't know. I don't remember them."

"Oh." She looked away awkwardly. "Sorry," she stammered.

I heard Kris's voice in my head. *Don't push people away. Not everyone is going to hurt you.* "It's okay," I told her. "It was a long time ago."

"Who do you live with?"

"My foster mom, Kris. She took me in a couple of years ago." I zipped up my makeup pouch. "How's volleyball?" I asked. "Still on the team?"

There was a long pause. "I quit, actually. Not because of my mark in art," she quickly added. "Other stuff. Friend stuff." She let out a long exhalation.

I was no expert on getting people to talk. Usually I was the one being prodded by someone else, but the way Jessica looked at me in the mirror was the way a drowning person would look at someone on shore. I was sure Kris had seen the same expression on my face a few times.

"Bad?" I asked.

"For me, it was."

"Some of those girls go out of their way to hurt people. You might be better off without them."

"Yeah, they turned on me pretty quick." There was no mistaking her bitter tone. "One of the guys in our group, he, um ... we were just fooling around, but he didn't stop when I said to ..."

"He assaulted you?" I asked.

She nodded. "It was about a month ago. I'd been drinking a little."

"That doesn't matter. You said no."

"I told one person and now she's blabbed to everyone. No one wants to believe Tyler Jefferies would do something like this."

Even I knew who Tyler Jefferies was. He and his crew were the male equivalent of Aprils: they walked around the school like rules didn't apply to them.

"Everyone's on his side. They're saying I made it up because I didn't tell anyone right away." Her voice dropped. "And that I'm a slut. That I wanted it."

"Shaming you," I said quietly. I knew how that worked, thanks to Foster Mom #2's Boyfriend #3.

"He's dating Sadie. The captain of the team. She's telling people I'm jealous and trying to break them up." Jessica snorted. "As if." She wiped her eyes. "I can't stand being near him."

I winced for Jessica. For what she'd gone through, and what she was going through.

She had a faraway look in her eye. "I barely sleep. I dropped out of volleyball, my grades suck ..." Her voice trailed off. "I wish I'd never said anything."

Everything she was saying hit close to home. I'd kept Boyfriend #3's secret because of his threats. When Kris had finally pried it out of me, I wished I'd told her sooner. The hundred-pound weight I'd been carrying around was suddenly gone. Well, maybe not gone, but sharing it with Kris had lightened the load. I hated that Jessica had done what she was supposed to do, confided in someone, and it had backfired.

"It's my word against his. I didn't go to a doctor. I should have, but I didn't. I just wanted to pretend it never happened. Now everyone thinks that proves I'm making it up."

"That's stupid. Anyone who's been through something like this knows that." The venom in my voice came fast. Jessica gave me a sharp look.

"Have you ...?" Her voice trailed off in a question.

I'd never admitted what happened to anyone other than Kris and a female cop. The recorded statement had been shown in court. Saying the words out loud to Jessica was too big a leap for me. As much as it might have helped her, I just couldn't do it.

The bell for first period rang. Jessica pulled herself together. "The worst part is going out there and facing everyone. I know they're talking about me, posting stuff. All the usual garbage." Jessica dabbed at her eyes and stared at herself in the mirror.

"You could skip bio. Hang out in here," I suggested.

She shook her head. "I can't miss any more classes. My parents are already hassling me about my grades. With all this going on, it's hard to concentrate on school."

"You didn't tell them about what happened?"

She scoffed. "No. It's too humiliating. They wouldn't understand."

I didn't know why Jessica should feel humiliated; none of it was her fault. But it wasn't my place to judge how things worked in her family.

"If you ever want to talk to someone, my foster mom specializes in this sort of thing." I let the offer hang between us. The self-portrait Jessica had done was making a lot more sense. I gave her another minute to collect herself and moved toward the door.

"Are you ready?" I asked her.

"Yeah." She took a deep, steadying breath, like a soldier ready to face the enemy. "Are you?"

I nodded. I'd had lots of practice dealing with Aprils, but Jessica hadn't. "I know we're not friends, but if you need anything, I'm around."

"Thanks," she said. "We're both going to bio, right? Maybe we can walk there together?"

In order to get there, we had to go past the bench under the trophy case. As we got closer, Jessica's steps slowed. A few Aprils were hanging out there, on a first period spare.

"I can't do it," Jessica said. She turned on her heel, ready to charge back to the washroom.

"Jessica!" I said, blocking her. "You can't hide out in there all day. You have nothing to be ashamed of. Don't let them do this to you." She started to shake her head. "I'll walk beside you. Trust me, they'll be so shocked at seeing us hanging out that they'll forget about the other stuff. For now, anyway."

That comment made her snort with laughter. "Good point." She bit her lip, thinking. "Okay. Let's get this over with."

As we got closer, the Aprils looked up from their phones and gave me the usual cursory glance, curling their glossy lips in distaste. It took them a moment to realize that the girl at my side was Jessica. "Oh my god," one of them said. "She showed up."

Jessica stiffened beside me, but kept walking. I wished that my armour could stretch into a force field to protect her, making all their comments bounce back onto them.

"Why is she with the goth freak?" another one said.

"Desperate much?" one cackled.

Neither of us said anything, but I could hear Jessica's shaky breathing. As soon as we were past them, she breathed a sigh of relief.

"You did it," I whispered.

When we got to Mr. Yeng's class, most of the kids had taken their seats. Jessica hesitated at the door, and I saw why. The girl she usually sat beside was glaring at her. "Come on," I said. "There's always a spot beside me."

For the rest of the day, I was Jessica's unofficial protector. We had art together, too, and at lunch, I showed her the Table of Death in the library. When the end of the day rolled around, I found her at her locker. "How're you doing?" I asked.

"I survived," she said. "Uh, so, tomorrow ..."

I was prepared for her to tell me leave her alone, that she didn't need my help.

"Can we meet in the washroom before school? Going past that bench on my own is too much." She cringed.

"Yeah, sure."

She gave me a grateful smile. "I couldn't have made it through today without you. Seriously. And, um ... can I get your number, in case I do want to talk to your foster mom?"

"Uh-huh," I said and tried to look chill about it. Being asked for your number wouldn't have been a big deal to most people. But no one had ever asked for mine before.

She thumbed my number into her phone and put it in her pocket. Her eyes fell on my ankh pendant. "That's cool," she said. "You're into Egyptian stuff?"

I looked down at it. "Sort of."

"My family's Egyptian," she said. "My grandpa's really into ancient history. He and my uncle have a stall at the Osborne Street flea market. They have all kinds of things like that." She gestured again to the pendant. She jammed the rest of her books into her bag. "Are you going that way?" she asked nodding to the front doors.

"Yeah."

"Me, too. I take the bus."

The halls were crowded with people and no one noticed us. I bit back a smile as we walked out of the front doors together.

"Hey, Frankie!" Max's voice caught me off guard as we walked down the school's front steps. He was leaning against the bike rack but moved onto the walkway and stood in front of us.

"Hi," I said. He eyed up Jessica and frowned. I hesitated before introducing him and then realized if I didn't, I was as bad as an April. "This is Jessica."

"Max," he said, and turned back to me. "I didn't think you had friends at this school."

"Max!" I hissed.

"What?" He held up his hands innocently. "It's what you told me."

Jessica laughed, unfazed by his rudeness. The bus came into view and pulled up to the stop. "See you tomorrow," she said.

As soon as she was out of earshot I turned on Max. "Why'd you say that?" I asked. "And why are you skulking around outside of school, anyway?"

He shrugged and didn't answer. There was an edge to him today. "Happy to have your phone back?" he asked. The way he asked made it sound like I should be more grateful. I bristled.

"Yeah. Thanks again for finding it." I tried to remember that he'd had a hard life and didn't have someone like Kris rooting for him. "Was there something else?" He was blocking my path. I either had to wait for him to move, or walk around him.

"I thought maybe we could hang out." He dug his hands into his hoodie pocket. The hopeful look on his face made him look even younger. A group of guys walked past us and snickered.

"Good luck, little dude," one said, laughing.

He glared after them.

"Sorry, I've got plans," I said. It wasn't a total lie, I wanted to tell Kris about Jessica and ask her advice. But

I also didn't feel like hanging out with Max. I was used to being a loner, and after spending the day with Jessica, I'd hit my socialization limit.

"Oh, yeah? What are they? Maybe I could join you."

I shook my head apologetically. "It's just me and Kris."

"What about tomorrow?"

"Maybe," I said, noncommittal. He stood waiting for me to say something else. "What?" I asked.

"Are you hanging out with Jessica?"

"I don't know, maybe." Was he jealous?

"So you just don't want to hang out with me."

Where is this attitude coming from? I shot him a pissed-off look and held up my hands, ready to walk away, but changed my mind. If he wanted the truth, I'd give it to him. "Honestly, being around you confuses me. Between the dreams and the stuff at the warehouse, I need to figure things out, and I don't think I can if we're hanging out."

His eyes turned fiery. "I confuse you?" he repeated. "I wish I could make things more clear," he said. His words were like broken glass. Each one of them had an edge to it.

"You're getting intense," I said. I barely knew the kid, but he acted like I owed him something.

"I should have known this would happen," he muttered angrily. He turned away, shaking his head, and dodged other kids in his race to leave.

"Scared away another one, huh?" an April jeered.

I gave her my most menacing glare and kept on staring until she got so uncomfortable that she hurried away with her friends.

"A girl from school might call you," I told Kris as we ate takeout sushi. I hadn't mentioned the awkward conversation with Max, and I didn't plan to. Thinking about him took the shine off the possibility that I had made a friend.

"How come?" Kris popped a piece of California roll in her mouth.

I explained the whole thing, even the part about walking past the Aprils on the bench. When I was done, Kris put down her chopsticks and looked at me. It was a heavy, serious look, and I worried I'd done something wrong, like maybe I shouldn't have given out my number or I'd broken Jessica's confidence by telling her story to Kris.

"May I hug you?" Kris asked.

"What?" I laughed. "Why?"

Kris took that as a yes and leaned over with her arms outstretched. "Because I'm proud of you, Frankie. Do you know how far you've come?"

When she said it like that, I guess I had come a long way from the rage-filled teenager she'd taken in. "And if you think it's because of me, it's not. I see how hard you're trying. At school and at everything else."

"Okay, stop it," I said and pushed her away. But under my makeup, my cheeks flushed with pride.

Later that night, the first photo appeared on my phone.

A message flashed on my screen from a number I didn't recognize. When I opened it, there was a photo of

Kris getting into her car. The location didn't look familiar, but it was definitely Kris.

I stared at the photo in shock, zooming in to catch every detail. She wasn't wearing the same clothes as she had on today. The photo could have been taken weeks ago, for all I knew. My body went numb. Was it a warning? Or a threat?

I jumped out of bed to show Kris, but when I got to her door, I heard her deep, rhythmic breathing. She was asleep. I stared at the photo once more. Who had sent it? And why?

And then, the weirdest thing happened. Before my eyes, the photo deleted itself. I tapped my messages, trying to pull it up again, but it was gone. My last received message was from five o'clock, when Kris had asked what I wanted for dinner.

I went back to my room, turned my phone off, and stuck it in my drawer. Getting a random photo of Kris was strange, but seeing it disappear before my eyes made me doubt if it had ever been there.

It took me a long time to fall asleep. When I finally did drift off, Frances's world was waiting for me.

24

WE WERE EATING AT LONG trestle tables under the stars. Bugs fought for space around the lanterns in the warm night air. "To Abeline!" Everyone raised their glasses, but not in celebration. Papa had found her in her tent that morning. Thor had dug the grave and carried her blanket-wrapped body over on his shoulder. We'd all followed in a grim procession.

I held no sentiment for Abeline. After the day that she'd mended my dress, I'd kept my distance, and she'd never shown any particular interest in me. I'd been surprised by the sorrow in Papa's voice as he gave her eulogy.

The funeral had brought back memories of Mama and the day she'd gone into the ground. I'd wanted to jump in with her, if only to lie with her one more time, to feel her hands stroking my hair, the beat of her heart against my cheek.

"Dead, and on today, of all days," Shirley harrumphed, pulling me away from the memory. I eyed her carefully across the dinner table. The ankh hung around my neck. I still didn't like it, but it was a gift from Papa so I wore it. Plus, I'd seen Ella stare at it jealously, which made it that much more appealing.

Yuri was sitting beside Papa. When the toast was done, he leaned over. "Perhaps we should change our plans. Change things to another night?" he suggested.

I looked between them, trying to follow the conversation. Papa glanced at me and then shook his head. "Hussein says it has to be on a full moon. I can't wait another month. Abeline wouldn't have wanted that," he said. I didn't know what Papa was talking about. Yuri's lips pressed into a thin line. He didn't like Papa's decision.

I glanced shyly at Mr. Hussein, wondering what part he played in Papa's plan. He'd been travelling with us for a while now, but he rarely spoke. He stared imperiously down his hook nose at the performers. Papa thought having a real Egyptian with the circus added mystique to the mummy. But Mr. Hussein's shifty eyes made me nervous, and I avoided sitting beside him.

Bowls of food were passed down the line as Papa rose again and spoke. "It is fitting that tonight we celebrate the life of our friend in a most unconventional way." Some of the performers paused midbite, forks suspended in the air as they listened. Concetta turned her dainty head to face Papa. Thor had been feeding her. He laid the fork down gently on her plate. "We will reconvene after dinner in the Mummy's Tent, where Mr. Hussein will begin our" — he paused, looking from performer to performer — "transformation."

Shirley sat at the end of the table, chewing on a chicken leg. "Everything's ready, then?"

I was confused. Everyone except me seemed to know what was going on.

"Mr. Hussein has prepared the mumia powder and assures me that it will work."

An excited twitter went up among the performers. I stared around, wide eyed. What was mumia powder? "Papa?"

"Shh." Papa put a hand on my shoulder and continued speaking. "Mr. Hussein? A few words?"

Mr. Hussein stood up. A hush fell over the table as we waited for him speak. He gave a slight bow to everyone at the table, but spoke directly to Papa. His voice was quiet and somber, his English stilted. "I must return to my homeland tomorrow. It is foretold by the heavens." He raised his hands up to the sky. "I have travelled a long way to bring you this gift. A blessed priest carries great power in Egypt. The power will be passed on to you through his bones. It will make you strong and invincible, keeping you healthy for years to come. It will make you —" he paused dramatically "— immortal!"

I watched Papa hold up his glass for a toast. *Immortal?* Was it possible? To live forever? Or was it some trick of the Egyptian man's? Papa was too smart for that, though, wasn't he? It was Papa who knew how to entice a crowd, thrill them with our peculiarities. Surely, he wouldn't have fallen victim to a hoax.

I looked at Mr. Hussein. His dark eyes glittered in the lantern light.

"And you're sure this will work?" Yuri asked.

"I carry the power of my ancestors," Mr. Hussein answered.

Yuri looked at Papa, one pale eyebrow raised skeptically. Papa's face hardened. "I believe in Hussein." He looked around the table, his eyes bright with determination. "You are all free to make your choice. No one will force you to join us. But I hope you know that whatever I do is with your best interests at heart. There is cruelty in this world. It is aimed at you. It was aimed at my beautiful Mathilde." He bowed his head at her name. "Perhaps if we had had the mumia powder then, she would still be with us. The world is not ready for you. We make our fortune off humanity's fascination with the peculiar, but I believe there will come a time when you are revered for the marvels that you are. My wish is for you to see that day."

The performers were silent when Papa sat down. A tear slid down Concetta's face, and Ahmed bowed his head to Papa. "It is an honour to perform in this circus," he murmured. Leopold nodded in agreement. The conversation after that was subdued. Everyone was lost in their own thoughts.

"Papa," I whispered. He was speaking with Yuri, but I was still confused. "Papa!"

"What is it?" He turned to me.

"If we drink the mumia powder, it means we can't die and we stay just as we are now?"

He nodded. "And no one will be able to hurt you."

"But Papa, I'll be a child forever."

"Yes. My angel forever." His eyes shone.

I opened my mouth to tell him Mama wanted to see me get married and have children of my own. No matter what Shirley had said about the chances of it happening, Mama had believed it would. A swell of frustration rose in my chest. Being a child forever sounded more like a curse than a blessing. "May I be excused?"

"You haven't finished your dinner," Papa said.

"I don't feel well," I said. Clumsily, I stood up and stepped over the bench. Wine glasses clinked as I bumped the table, upsetting them. The other performers watched in surprise.

"Frances?" Papa's concerned voice followed me as I took off at a run to our wagon.

I threw myself down on my cot with a heaving sob.

"Frances?" a voice called from outside. But it wasn't Papa. It was Gus. Still not welcome at the performers' table, he ate by himself. His lantern swung, casting a long shadow on the canvas walls.

"Go away," I cried.

"What's wrong?"

"You wouldn't understand."

"I'll stay here until you tell me," he said stubbornly. "Please, Miss Frances?" He'd gotten good at impersonating the performers, and his imitation of Concetta's sweet voice was spot-on. But I wasn't in the mood.

"Let me be."

It was quiet for a few minutes. I thought he'd left, but then he called, "You stopped crying. Can I come in now?" Faithful Gus. He'd stay by my side forever, if I let him.

When I didn't argue, he opened the flap and stuck his head inside. I turned a tear-stained face toward him. "What happened?" he asked.

"I — I can't tell you."

"Because I'm not a performer?" His voice had a bitter edge.

I nodded.

"Well, you don't have to, because I already know."

"You do?"

Gus hesitated. "It's about that mummy and Mr. Hussein, isn't it?"

My eyes widened in surprise. "How did you find out?"

He climbed up into the wagon and put the lantern down on the trunk at the end of my bed. I moved over so there was room for him to sit on my cot. "I heard him and your papa talking in the tent where they keep the mummy. He was grinding something up with a mortar and pestle, like what Yuri uses to make his remedies. Mr. Hussein said it was to be mixed into the water, and then everyone would go to sleep like normal, but wake up as something else. After they left, I snuck in to have a look. And guess what?" He leaned closer, his eyes wide. "Part of that mummy is missing. I think that's what Mr. Hussein was grinding up!"

I stared at Gus, my mind clicking through all the pieces. "We're supposed to drink that powder. That's what Papa said. It'll give us everlasting life."

Gus's excitement about his secret faded. His face paled. "When?"

"Tonight." I hesitated, unsure if I should tell him everything. "It's because of Mama. How she died. He doesn't want anyone else to get hurt because of how we look. Because of what we are." *The world is not kind to people like us.*

"I'd never hurt you," he said with quiet intensity. "I think you're beautiful."

My heart thumped in my chest. "You do?"

"You're like a fairy tale. A cursed princess." His voice was tender. He put a finger to my cheek and stroked it. A shiver ran down to my toes. No one had ever touched me like that before.

"I don't want to drink it," I confided.

"Why not?"

"Because. I'll be a child forever. I don't want that! Do you?"

Gus frowned. "It doesn't matter. Your papa won't let me drink it. I'm not one of you. You're all going to leave without me, anyway."

I shook my head. "No! We'd never do that."

Gus's face settled into a sulk. "I heard him plain as day tell Thor that you're picking up and going to Europe. 'We'll have to get rid of the extra baggage,' he said. I didn't know what he meant at the time, but now I do. He meant me and the horses."

No Gus? But he was my only true friend. I couldn't leave him! "But —" I stammered, "you're all I've got!"

His back stiffened. "Do you care about me, Frances?"

"You know I do. You're my best friend."

He faced me. "I don't want to leave you."

"Then don't! We'll convince Papa that I need you with me. I'll think of something."

"What if I drank the mumia? If I was like you, we couldn't be separated. He'd have to take me. Imagine seeing the world." He had a dreamy look in his eyes. "It wouldn't matter that we were children. We'd be together, forever."

"But what if it's a trick? Or poison?" Something about Mr. Hussein still didn't sit right with me.

Gus frowned. "Your papa wouldn't do that to his performers."

That was true. Papa would never put them in danger. "How, then? How would we do it?"

Gus looked across the tent at a chair with tomorrow's dress laid out on it. Abeline had washed and dried it. One of her last chores before she'd passed. "I'll dress up as you."

Laughter burst out of me. "As a girl?"

Gus shrugged. "Why not? I'm only a little taller than you. Concetta has all kinds of wigs. I can borrow one with blond hair. If I keep my head down, no one will notice. After I drink the wine, you can step into the tent. By then it will be too late. Of course, your papa will let you drink as well. He would never leave you behind."

"If Papa discovers —"

"I'm out no matter what! This is my only chance!" Gus squeezed my hand hard enough to make me wince. "Don't leave me, Frances. I have no one else."

The desperation in his voice was heartbreaking. From the day that I'd found him hiding like a scruffy, hungry puppy, I'd known that he needed me. If we left him alone, what would happen? He'd be another orphan living hand to mouth and begging for scraps. Or worse, sent back to the boys' home and then to a factory to live a short, miserable life.

"All right," I sighed.

He gave me a triumphant smile. "One day, we'll have our own circus. Me and you, travelling the world together."

"Our own?" I stared at him incredulously, looking to see if he was teasing. His eyes shone with ambition. "But Papa —"

Gus waved impatiently. "Don't worry about him. One day, he'll be ready to step aside."

The circus was Papa's life, his *raison d'être*, as he liked to say. Besides me, the circus was all that he had.

"I don't think he'd ever be ready to do that."

"No?" Gus tilted his head at me and shrugged. "We'll see."

A silhouette appeared on the canvas wall of the wagon a moment before Papa put his head inside. He frowned when he saw Gus. "Get out!" he said, his voice wound tight.

Gone was Gus's bravado as he scrambled to grab his lantern and slink past Papa, but Papa grabbed him by his shirt collar and hauled him back. "You shouldn't be in here."

Gus's eyes widened with fear, and he gave a quick nod, then raced away, his lantern light bobbing. But I'd seen a flash of something else in his eyes as he left. Defiance, maybe. I didn't have time to think about it. I spun away from Papa and stared at the cabinet card of Mama propped up on my washstand. It was from her younger days, and she was smiling sweetly, holding her skirts up slightly to reveal the toes of one of the extra feet. My heart lurched at the sight of her. Some days the pain was numbed, but tonight it came on in full force.

"Frances," Papa began. He sat down heavily on my cot, making the rope strings under the thin mattress groan. "I suppose I should have told you about Hussein earlier. Given you some time to understand it."

I crossed my arms tightly against my chest. I was still upset.

"Everything I'm doing is for you. I'm trying to keep this circus alive for you. We used to play the best vaude-ville houses in the country. We'd pack them! And now look at us. Playing for country people, dragging our-selves over dirt roads to make a living. This isn't the life I want for you."

I looked at him, confused.

"Imagine: The Circus of the Undead! Imagine the ways we could shock the audience, the stunts we could perform! It will take some time, some practice to reinvent ourselves, but the story is too delicious. People will come from all over to see if it's true. We'll get back into the best theatres. No more setting up in dusty fields, travelling for days between towns." He got down on his knees in front of me and grabbed my hands in his. "And my Alligator Girl will be the jewel in the crown, the ageless, youthful angel who will bring in audiences from all around the world.

Lantern light flickered across Papa's face. His eyes shone with excitement. The way he spoke made my worries drift away. How could I stay mad at him?

"You'll come tonight," he said, part question, part demand, "to the Mummy's Tent. We will all drink the mumia powder together and begin our journey. We will be reborn, Frances." His eyes wandered again to Mama's cabinet card. "You're all I have now that she's gone." My reservations melted away.

"I'll wear one of my white dresses," I said to Papa. My promise to Gus was in the back of my mind. "They're your favourite, aren't they? I'll look pretty for you."

He smiled, relief plain on his face. "Yes. That will be perfect," he said with a sigh. He held me a few minutes longer, then left. He had preparations to make. I looked at Mama's picture as if it could give me an answer, and I wondered what would become of us.

I woke up sweating. I took my phone out of the drawer and turned it on to check the time. Three in the morning, and I was wide awake. Images from Frances's world swirled in my head. I fumbled in the dark to turn on the lamp and grab my sketchbook. The drawings came quickly, pouring out of me and onto the paper. When I looked at my phone next, three hours had passed.

I still didn't know why Frances's memories were being revealed to me. What was my connection to her? Was it our skin, or the ankh? I supposed one way to find out would be to give the ankh away, but what if I couldn't get the dreams back? I needed to know what happened to Frances and the circus.

As I sat sketching, my phone vibrated. I flipped it over. Another photo of Kris. This time, she was at the grocery store. I'd been hoping I'd imagined the first one. But here was another one. Was it going to disappear as well? *Who are you?* I texted.

Three dots appeared as a response was typed. *We're waiting for you.*

Before I could take a screenshot, the message and the photo disappeared.

What was going on? I didn't like that someone had control of my phone, or that they had followed Kris. Was someone trying to be funny? Max, maybe? But there was nothing funny about the photos, or the message. If anything, it felt like I was being stalked.

The chain of events that had led to my phone disappearing and then magically reappearing weren't coincidental. I hadn't been afraid of Monsieur Duval when I'd seen him onstage, but maybe I should have been. What if the shows had been his way of giving me a false sense of security? It was eerily similar to Foster Mom #2's Boyfriend #3. He'd done a good job of making me feel safe. Until all of a sudden, I wasn't.

25

"EARLY MEETING," Kris said as she rushed by me to fill her travel mug. I was in my pyjamas, sketching at the kitchen table. I'd tried going back to sleep, but it had been a wasted effort. Kris was in her work clothes, and her bag was packed and ready to go by the back door. "And, of course, I slept in," she groaned. She was like a human tornado whirling past me.

"Kris, last night —"

"More dreams?" she asked, grabbing a banana.

"No. Someone sent some photos." That made her pause and look at me. "They were of you. Like someone was following you."

Her eyebrows shot up. "Let me see."

"That's what's weird. Whoever sent them was able to make them disappear. Like they do on Snapchat, except it was just sent as a normal text." Even though I knew the photos and texts were gone, I unlocked the phone and handed it to her.

She did all the things that I'd done, scrolling through my settings to Privacy and Location.

"The case I've been working on," she said, "it's really complicated. Someone involved could be trying to intimidate me."

It hadn't occurred to me that the photos might not have had anything to do with the circus. "Seriously?"

Kris nodded. "Yeah."

"It's working," I said. "Who are these guys?"

She shook her head. "You know I can't talk about it. It's an active case."

"Kris," I started. The idea of her being in danger sent a wave of panic through me. She saw it on my face.

"I didn't tell you to scare you," she reassured me. "I'll get the police to look into it."

"How did they get my number?"

"These guys are well connected."

She put my phone down on the counter. I stared at it like it was possessed. "What should I do?"

"Turn it off and leave it at home," Kris said. She checked the time on her watch and let out a panicked groan. "I've got to go. You're okay?"

I nodded, but it wasn't me I was worried about. "Kris," I said, watching her sling her bag onto her shoulder, "be careful."

She grinned and winked at me. "I always am." But before she turned away, I saw the smile change into a frown.

"Take this." Jessica held out her phone to me. We'd met in the washroom as planned. "Seriously. It's like carrying around a loaded gun. I keep checking it, and the posts are just getting worse." She tapped in her passcode and showed me what was being written about her.

I was no prude, but even I was horrified. "Jessica," I gasped.

"Yeah. Nice friends, huh? It's like a big pile-on. One person says something online, and then you're fair game. People who don't even know me are calling me a liar and ... other things."

I knew how it felt not to be believed. Kris called it the "shame and blame" game. It was easier for some people to pretend that a bad thing hadn't happened or to blame the victim than to admit the ugly truth about someone who was so "likeable" or "popular."

"Why were you reading them?"

"I don't know. I couldn't stop. I thought it would be worse not knowing, but then ..." She took a deep, shaky breath. "I thought walking past the girls yesterday was bad, but today it's going to be even worse. I don't think I can face them."

"You can't stay in here forever," I reminded her.

Jessica shook her head. "You don't know what it's like!"

My throat went dry because I did know what it was like.

It was hard, even now, years later, to think about it. All I had to do was close my eyes and I was back at Foster Mom #2's, stuck in a room with him: Boyfriend #3. I'd known what he was doing was wrong, but I'd been too afraid to say anything. During the darkest times with Foster Mom #2, sessions with Kris had been a bright spot. For an hour each week, I felt like someone cared.

She'd pulled every string she could to get me away from that foster mom and into her own care. Seeing Jessica's pain now reminded me what a relief it had been to finally tell someone — and to be believed.

The bell for first period rang, and Jessica shot me a panicked look.

"We'll go to bio and art together, and then you can sneak into film studies with me for third period. Mr. Nham is showing *Apocalypse Now*. He won't even know you're there. You can hear him snoring over the soundtrack. We can ditch at lunch to avoid the cafeteria."

Jessica looked so grateful that I thought she might start crying.

The highlight of bio was when it finished. My hand ached from writing three pages of notes. It was like Mr. Yeng was in a contest for least inspiring teacher of the year. Max hadn't shown up, and I doubted he'd be in art class, either, but I scanned the hallway for him, anyway. As much as I didn't want another awkward run-in with him, I was curious to ask if he was the one who'd sent the photos. I didn't spot him, though, and was pleased when Jessica took the seat beside me in art.

Mr. Kurtis rubbed his hands together, impatient for us to get settled in. He was sitting on his stool at the front of the class. "New assignment," he said. "Inspired by Frankie."

"Me?" A few kids turned in my direction.

Mr. Kurtis nodded. "Your assignment is to play around with the graphic novel."

There was the usual mutterings and a few groans. "Does it have to be funny?" a guy asked.

Mr. Kurtis shook his head. "Graphic novels aren't the same as comic books. Anyone know the difference?" Ms. O'Brian had asked the same thing in English when we started reading *Persepolis*.

A few hands went up, including Jessica's. He called on her first.

"A graphic novel is just like a book, only the illustrations help tell the story, too."

"Exactly," Mr. Kurtis said. "What else?"

"You can do speech bubbles and stuff like that," someone else said.

"Uh-huh. What I really like, as an art teacher, is that you can explore perspective, angle, and style with this assignment. I want you to take an experience you've had and turn it into a one-page graphic story. Pick something personal, something you can really dig your teeth into. Before we get started, take a look at some of these." He pointed to a stack of books on the front table. "See which ones you're drawn to. Make a list of the things you notice as you go through the books. How would you describe the style of the art? Is it in colour or black and white?" He posted a bunch of questions on the SMART Board. "I've also got templates that you can use to map out the story. Remember, it's one page only!"

While the other kids flipped through the graphic novels at the front, Mr. Kurtis made his way over and pulled his stool up to my desk. "I think you've got a handle on this," he said with a smile. "While the other kids work on their one-pagers, you can keep going with your project. You want to show me what you've done?"

I passed him my sketchbook so he could start at the beginning. Jessica had gone up to the pile of books and came back with three, which she spread out in front of her. But she quickly abandoned them so she could check out my drawings, too. She was leaning so close to me that I pushed my chair back so she could move into my spot. It gave me a nervous thrill, watching their eyes skim the pages. I looked for some sign that Mr. Kurtis loved or hated it, but he kept his face expressionless. Jessica's reaction was easier to gauge. She beamed at me and made little gasping noises at certain parts. I hadn't warned her about Mathilde's attack, and when she got to that part, she stiffened.

When they reached the last frame, Mr. Kurtis ran a hand through his hair and let out a huge exhalation. I held my breath, waiting for his pronouncement. "Amazing!" He slapped the cover. A few kids looked over. "Best work you've done all year. The character development and facial features ... these characters feel real. I love the perspective shifts in each scene. And the attention to detail ..." He shook his head, at a loss for words. "You must have done a lot of research. Whatever happens when they drink that potion is the big climactic scene. What about Frances? What's her big moment going to be? Her critical choice?"

I didn't want to tell him that I had no idea until I fell asleep and dreamed it. "You'll have to wait and see," I said and bit back a grin.

Mr. Kurtis laughed and stood up.

"Teacher's pet," Jessica whispered after he'd walked away. I rolled my eyes at her.

By the time we were halfway through class, Jessica had a few things down on her template. Was she drawing what I thought she was drawing?

"Jessica?" I raised my eyebrows.

"He said he wanted something personal."

The first square had her crying on a bed, with her knees pulled up to her face. In the next, a guy was laughing and getting backslapped by his friends.

In the third, she was getting ghosted by her friends at school.

In the fourth, a girl in the washroom was handing her a tissue. Her eyes, ringed with eyeliner, were filled with concern.

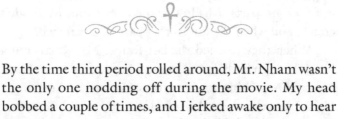

By the time third period rolled around, Mr. Nham wasn't the only one nodding off during the movie. My head bobbed a couple of times, and I jerked awake only to hear Mr. Nham snoring and see that half the class were on their phones. No one was paying attention to the movie except a couple of kids sitting at the front.

Jessica had decided to go to her English class after all, and I'd promised to meet her in "our" washroom at lunch. But getting through film studies was more of a challenge than I thought. After resting my chin on my hand and trying to focus on the movie one more time, I realized I had to give in to sleep. It didn't occur to me that I might dream about Frances at school, but that was what happened.

Gus waited impatiently while I buttoned up the back of the dress, my fingers working as quickly as they could. "Do you think it will hurt?" I asked him.

"How could it? It's just a drink."

"Not the drinking, silly. Becoming immortal."

"Even if it does, I don't care." Gus turned, and the pearl button I was working on slipped out of my fingers. He held my hand in his and gently squeezed. "Whatever happens, we'll be together. Forever." His eyes shone in the darkness. "One day, I'll own my own circus, just like your papa. I'll call it Gus's Circus of Wonder Children. You'll be my star performer."

"Me?"

"Yes! The beautiful Alligator Girl with the skin of a reptile and the soul of an angel. I'll tell the story of how you rescued me, a destitute street urchin, and brought me into the circus."

"And how you rose to become the ringmaster!" I finished.

It was a lovely fairy tale, and it distracted me from what we were doing.

"All the acts will be children. Now that we know about the mumia powder, we'll make them drink it, too. A whole troupe of us, children forever."

"How long have you been thinking about this?" I asked, frowning. It was a very well-drawn-out plan for someone who'd just found out about the mumia powder.

"I've always thought you should be the headlining act. The way Monsieur Duval makes you into a wild thing scares people. He needs to show the real you, not the fake one. The audience would fall in love with you. Like Concetta. When she sings, the audience forgets she's a limbless woman. All they hear is her voice. The part about it just being children came to me after your papa made me leave your wagon."

I was about to remind him that if it hadn't been for Papa, he'd still be out on the street, but he turned around so I could keep buttoning the dress. "You've given this a lot of thought," I said quietly, "haven't you?"

"Not a lot. Just …" His voice trailed off. "Forever is a long time. We'll have to make plans to give ourselves a reason to keep going."

A cold, hard lump settled in my stomach.

"Almost done? It must be getting close to midnight." He sounded impatient.

"Last one," I said. Together, we slipped out of my wagon. The moon hung in a perfect orb as Gus and I snuck between the tents. Despite my nerves, I had to stifle a laugh. He looked ridiculous in my white dress. His shoulders were too broad, and it pulled across the back. His legs poked out of the bottom, and my shoes were too small for him, so he was barefoot. I'd never noticed how bowlegged he was. The wig we'd stolen from Concetta's tent sat crookedly on his head, curls bouncing as he ran.

The tent with the mummy lay just ahead of us, lit from the inside with candlelight. As we got closer, I could hear excited murmurs. They were all in there, waiting for me. The picnic table we'd been eating at earlier was littered with glasses and plates; no one had bothered to clean up.

"We have to wait for Frances," Concetta wailed. "Where is she?"

"She's coming," Papa reassured her, but there was worry in his voice.

His shadow grew larger as he walked toward the tent flap. Gus ducked out of sight just in time. Papa opened his mouth to call for me again, but stopped abruptly when he saw me. "There you are!"

I resisted the urge to glance back at Gus. I could feel his hungry eyes staring at me as I followed Papa into the tent. *You'll be in here soon enough*, I thought.

"Let us begin," Papa said, ushering me to stand beside him. I looked around. Candles sat in holders along the sides of the tent, casting long shadows. A lantern at the front glowed. The mummy lay in its sarcophagus on the raised platform behind Mr. Hussein, who stood at a table with enough glasses for everyone, and a pitcher of water. There was a small brass container with a lid. It must have held the mumia powder. He wore his usual white robe and tasselled hat, and in his hands he held an ankh, just like my pendant.

Yuri caught my eye and winked. To him, this was a bit of fun. I could see it in his eyes. I also saw Tabitha staring at Yuri with moony eyes. I'd caught her doing this often, and I understood now that that was the look you gave someone you loved. Ahmed stood at the end of the line.

"Let's get on with it," Shirley mumbled, making it clear she didn't believe in all the mumbo jumbo. Ella and Elvira threw irritated glances at her. The twins had never liked Shirley. Papa looked around and nodded for Mr. Hussein to begin. The lump in my stomach jumped to my throat, and I grabbed for Papa's hand. But instead of finding comfort in its warmth, I found it as cold and damp with sweat as my own.

Mr. Hussein had a book in front of him. It looked ancient, with curled parchment pages and indecipherable writing. He held his hands out to either side, raised them to the sky, and began chanting in another language. His voice was nasally and stuck in his throat. Some of the performers closed their eyes. Others, like Daniel and

Leopold, watched Mr. Hussein, their eyebrows arched in suspicion.

I met Yuri's eyes. He gave me another wink as if to assure me there was nothing to worry about. I felt myself relax. Perhaps this was all for fun, like the hot summer nights when we went swimming in streams in moonlight. Or had champagne toasts at the end of a successful run in a town. Mama's death had put an end to frivolities like that. Maybe this was Papa's way of rekindling what we'd lost.

Mr. Hussein stopped talking and bowed to the mummy as if in gratitude, then he turned back to the table in front of him. He took the lid off the brass container and scooped a spoonful of what looked to be black ashes into each of the thirteen glasses in front of him, then filled each one with water. The mumia powder made it murky. The air inside the tent grew tense as Papa stepped up to the table and took two glasses, one for me and one for him. Daniel went next, taking glasses for himself and Concetta, then Ella and Elvira. Leopold waddled up, his chin barely grazing the tabletop, and reached for a glass. Mr. Hussein had to push it closer for him to grab. Yuri took one and brought one to Shirley. She made a long, irritated exhalation and held the glass against her stomach while Tabitha, Thor, and Ahmed collected theirs.

I stared into my glass and then back at the mummy. I couldn't see it from where I stood, but I wondered what part Mr. Hussein had ground up. Gus had said some of the mummy was missing, but I hadn't thought to ask what part. Was it an arm? A finger? I curled my lips at the thought of drinking the liquid. It smelled chalky, and powder drifted down to the bottom of the glass. I glanced at Papa beside me. His chin was set with determination.

Mr. Hussein began chanting in his language. He pointed the ankh at each of us, as if anointing us with its power. He raised his arms, and his voice grew louder. The tent had become stuffy with so many bodies, but I felt myself getting swept up in the moment, my body moving to the rhythm of the words. Ella and Elvira turned their dreamy eyes to Mr. Hussein, their Clara-Bow lips slightly parted in perfect Os, and closed their eyes. Beside me, I felt Yuri start to sway, his eyes shut. I kept mine open, watching as Mr. Hussein stretched his arms out wide, carried away by the majesty of his own voice.

The candle flames flickered, and a few went out. Elvira opened her eyes and looked around, startled, but the rest of the troupe was oblivious. A chill crept into the tent, like a dark shadow had joined us. I dropped Papa's hand. Behind me, I heard a rustle. I waited until Elvira closed her eyes again and took a small step backwards. In the dim light, another person my size with blond hair and a white dress would pass for me. That was what we were counting on.

I took another step back. Everyone was too entranced by Mr. Hussein's voice to pay any attention to me. As I slid closer to the tent flap, Gus and I exchanged positions. He stood to the left of Papa, far enough back that he'd be in Papa's peripheral vision, but not close enough to be identified as an imposter. I moved into the night, swallowed up by the darkness outside, and watched.

Mr. Hussein kept his hands raised to the sky as his voice grew louder still, the chant speeding up. I felt it then, like a serpent twisted around my throat — the same feeling I'd had when the men had found Mama in the woods. I hadn't known what it was then.

But I did now. Dread.

I woke with a start. A puddle of saliva had collected on the desk. Gross. I wiped it away with my sleeve. The credits rolled on the screen as the class packed up, most of them bleary eyed. I couldn't leave my desk until I'd sketched what had happened in my dream. Mr. Kurtis was right. Frances's big moment was coming.

26

W HEN I GOT TO THE WASHROOM, I hesitated. I wouldn't have been surprised if Jessica wasn't there. I'd drawn the dream in quick, broad strokes, but it had still made me ten minutes later than our agreed upon time. Tendrils of Frances's dream world still clung to me as I pushed open the door. I had a moment of doubt that Jessica wouldn't be there. She'd have found someone else to hang out with, or gotten tired of waiting.

Not only was she still there, but so were a couple of Aprils. I took in the scene before me. Jessica was cornered, but she was holding her own. She looked more pissed off than scared. I cleared my throat.

The two Aprils turned. One took a step away from Jessica, the other glared at me. "Your new bestie?" she asked Jessica. "Or is it beastie?" She snorted at her own joke.

I went toward her with my hands out and ready to grab, strangle, or slap. Her shriek pierced the air, but it was Jessica's shout of "No!" and the way she lunged to get between me and the April that made me stop. "She's not worth it!" Jessica yanked on my jacket, pulling me away from her.

"Watch your back!" I snarled at her as Jessica opened the door and dragged me into the hallway.

"Watch yours!" she said before the door closed.

"What was she saying to you?" I asked, still fired up.

"The same stuff as online. She just said it to my face." Jessica had done a good job of holding herself together, but I could tell she was rattled. We walked toward the front entrance. Getting out of school for the afternoon was a good idea. I was afraid of what I'd do if I saw that April from the washroom again.

"Where do you want to go?" I asked.

"Starbucks?" Jessica asked. I shook my head. It would be crawling with Aprils. "Mall?" she suggested, less enthusiastically. Again, not my scene. Then her face lit up. "We could visit my grandpa at the flea market. He's always bugging me to come by. You'll like it if you're into Egyptian stuff."

I said yes without hesitation. Compared to overpriced coffee or the mall, the flea market sounded perfect.

The Osborne Street flea market was a few blocks from school. Along the way, Jessica told me that her grandpa had owned the stall since he'd retired. Now that he was getting older, her uncle did most of the work. "Grandpa still goes in every day, though. I think he likes chatting with the people at the other stalls." The entrance to the flea market was through a set of double doors marked by a hand-drawn sign. *Flea Market this way.*

The tables were laid out in orderly rows along the walls. Some were covered with junk, but a few had legitimate collectibles and antiques and were set up more like a store than a garage sale. Some of the stalls were permanent, with dividers set up to make the space more private. The whole place had a slightly unpleasant odour, like everything had been sitting in a musty basement for too long.

Jessica and I made our way past a stall filled with needlepoint pictures and precariously stacked porcelain teacups. A sneeze would have brought everything crashing to the floor. Farther down, there was a guy selling vintage concert T-shirts and records, as well as some superhero dolls. I looked longingly at the figure of Wonder Woman and thought about buying it for Kris. As it was a Thursday afternoon, there were only a few people milling around.

Jessica directed me to a stall tucked in a corner at the far end of the room. It had a table in front, and partitions created a small room in the back. Jessica hadn't been joking when she said her grandfather and uncle were interested in Egypt. The stall was like a museum, filled with bronze statues of cats, posters from travelling exhibits of Egyptian mummies, and colourful paintings of gods on papyrus. I wouldn't have been surprised to find a sarcophagus hiding under the table. A bent-backed man shuffled out of the little room and sat down in his chair. He turned on a desk lamp and inspected something under the light. Jessica grinned and elbowed me. "That's my grandpa." A few strands of hair were combed over his age-spot-speckled baldness.

We moved closer, and I cleared my throat. On the walk over, I'd warned Jessica that old people usually hated me. They'd cross the street when they saw me coming. One might have thought that people closer to death would understand goth culture more than young people did, but it didn't work that way. I guess the closer you got to death, the less you wanted to think about it.

He looked up, peering at us through his glasses. It took him a moment to realize it was his granddaughter standing in front of him. "Jessica! You came to surprise me!" he said in accented English. He stood up and shuffled around to the front of the table so he could hug her. "You don't have school today?" he asked.

"We're doing research for an art project," Jessica answered, cleverly evading his question. "About Egypt." Which wasn't a total lie.

His face lit up.

"This is my friend Frankie." Jessica turned to me. "Frankie, my grandpa, Tomar Ibrahim."

There was a second of hesitation as his eyes skirted over my black clothes, makeup, and purple hair, but then he held out his hand. "Any friend of Jessica's is a friend of mine." It sounded like he was forcing himself to believe it, but he gave me a kind smile.

"Is Uncle Fahid here?" Jessica had told me about him, too. Her mother's older brother had recently moved back home to help run the booth.

Mr. Ibrahim shook his head. "He comes in after lunch, and I go home. I'm getting too old for these long days. So, what is the project? How can I help?" His eyes crinkled in a smile as he peered at us over his glasses. Age spots dotted his cheeks and forehead, too. His hands trembled a bit, due to age, not fear. I was close enough that I could smell the scent of old, dry paper on him. Dust from the relics hung heavy in the air. "I have this ankh," I said, lifting the pendant to show him. "I know it means something different than what they usually mean —"

I stopped talking because his face had completely transformed. "Where did you get this?"

"Someone gave it to me when I was little. I don't remember who."

Mr. Ibrahim breathed out like he was in pain. "This is a talisman. It's very big magic."

"Big magic?" I repeated.

He formed his hands into fists. "*Dark* is a better word, maybe."

"What does it do?"

"It captures the souls of the dead."

That was exactly what Monsieur Duval had told Frances when he gave it to her.

"Come, I will show you." He gestured for us to move out of the aisle and into the stall. "Sit." Jessica pulled over a chair from a desk at the back, and I took the one closer to her grandfather.

Mr. Ibrahim hauled a massive book out from under his table and thumped it down on top. The lamplight shook in its wake. Gold letters on the dusty cover read, *Encyclopedia of Antiquities.* He flipped through the pages, licking his thumb as he went. "Here!" He jabbed his finger at a picture. I leaned closer as he angled the book toward me. "You see? The point on the bottom changes the ankh." He said *ankh* with a thick, hard ending. "The Egyptians believed that for a soul to live on, it had to be able to find a body. This was why they mummified people. But if a body could not be mummified, an ankh like this would serve the purpose. Rather than leaving a soul to wander, an Egyptian priest could attach it to this ankh. Like I said, it's dark magic. Difficult magic."

I caught Jessica looking at her grandpa with a hint of a smile. It might have sounded like a folk tale to her, but not to me.

"Have you ever heard of mumia powder?" I asked.

He snorted. "Oh, yes!" He yanked open a desk drawer. My heart skipped a beat. Was he going to pull out a jar of it?

I relaxed when he put a framed photograph on the table in front of us. It was black and white and showed two men. One was wearing a fez and a white robe. The other man wore suspenders and khaki pants, and since he was taller, he was resting his arm on the other man's shoulders. The desert stretched out behind them, sand dunes and everything. "You see these men? This is Jessica's great-grandfather, Ashrif." He pointed to the one wearing the white robe. "He was an archaeologist. This man" — he pointed to the other — "is Terrence Scott." Mr. Ibrahim looked at us like we should know who he was. "A famous Egyptologist. This was taken in 1922. The same year Carter found King Tutankhamun's tomb. You know who he is?" he asked me. I nodded.

"All of a sudden, Egyptian antiquities became playthings. They had mummy unwrapping parties! Can you imagine? Bodies preserved for a millennium were dug up and sold. It was a desecration! Tomb robbers made a fortune. But not Ashrif. He and Scott wanted to preserve what they found. Their dream was to start a museum *in* Egypt to house their finds." He turned a page in his book to show a decorated sarcophagus heavy with gold leaf. The stylized face of an Egyptian man had been drawn on the top. "They discovered this tomb. At first, they thought it was a pharaoh's. The wealth inside was staggering, but as they read the hieroglyphs on the wall, they realized it belonged to a priest. A priest who had been buried like a king. He must have been very powerful to deserve such treasure." He shot me a look as if I should know where he was going.

"But Terrence and Ashrif discovered that a curse had been put upon the body of the mummy. Indeed, the whole tomb was a cursed place. They decided to seal it back up and leave the priest's body untouched."

His eyes flashed. "But not everyone obeyed. Ashrif's brother saw the fortune they'd walked away from. He robbed the tomb and stole everything, including the mummy. He sailed across the ocean with it."

"What happened to it?" I asked. *Don't let that be the end of the story.* I finally felt like I was getting somewhere.

He tapped his fingers on the table. "Where is it?" he muttered to himself, looking around. Standing up, he opened a few boxes and sifted through news clippings. "Ah!" Triumphantly, he held up a flyer, aged and yellowed by time. "Found it." *Monsieur Duval's Circus of Marvels and Wonders*, the old newspaper ad read. I stared at it, not trusting myself to speak. "I think this was where the mummy ended up."

He pointed to the bottom of the ad. *Come one and all to see a real Egyptian mummy! Will you be pure of heart and survive the curse?* I stared at him, incredulous.

"Why do you think it's the same mummy?" I asked.

A slow smile spread across his face. He pulled another photo from the pile. It was a photo of Monsieur Duval's circus. Frances was in it, and so was Mr. Hussein. "Because *he* was my great-uncle."

27

I WAS GLAD THAT I WAS ALREADY sitting down. "Did you ever meet him?" I asked.

"Oh, yes." Mr. Ibrahim nodded. "He lived with my family. It was while he was on his deathbed that he told me the story of the cursed mummy."

"Can you tell us about it?" I asked.

Beside me, Jessica muttered something like, "Curses *again*."

"As I said, at that time, it was fashionable to have mummy unwrapping parties, or to grind up a part of the mummy into a fine powder."

"Mumia powder," I murmured.

He nodded. "People thought it would cure all manner of ills. Some thought there was special power in the body of a mummy." He shook his head angrily. "It was a desecration to do this, but like anything, if there was money to be made ..." He held up his hands in a helpless gesture. "My great-uncle Hussein was an educated man. He could read the hieroglyphs and had studied the *Book of the Dead*, but he was also greedy and saw an opportunity. I have no idea if his story was true, but he claimed that the mumia powder made from the priest gave immortality."

"Do you think that's possible?"

Jessica snorted and rolled her eyes, so I knew what she thought.

Mr. Ibrahim regarded me. "I have learned a lot since sitting by my great-uncle's bedside. I have passed on what I could to Jessica's uncle Fahid. The passage to everlasting life is complicated, but the Egyptians believed it was possible. They left records of what had to be done. The *Book of the Dead*, as English scholars call it, really should have been translated as the *Book of Life*. It was like a manual for how to get to the afterlife. Most Egyptians lived in order to die. They believed the afterlife was the reward for enduring mortality." Mr. Ibrahim paused. "Make sense so far?" he asked. I nodded, but Jessica's attention had wandered. She'd probably heard all of this before.

"As for mumia powder, it was like a secret ingredient, *if* the body had been prepared properly. And all the elements — air, fire, earth, water, and ether — had to be present."

"What's ether?" I asked.

"A well-intentioned spirit. It was believed that only with those five things could the world of imperfection, life, be altered to the world of perfection, afterlife. In other words, immortality on earth."

"And if all those things were present, then what? Would the powder work?"

"It's the stuff of legend. Like the philosopher's stone, or the Holy Grail. But —" he paused "— legend is often based on truth."

A shadow fell across the desk. I looked up … and thought I was staring into the eyes of Mr. Hussein.

The man in front of me had the same hooked nose and deep-set eyes, but he was older and bald, and instead of wearing a robe, he had a blazer over a button-down shirt tucked into jeans. It wasn't Mr. Hussein; it was Jessica's uncle.

"Ah, Fahid!" said Mr. Ibrahim. "Look who came by! Jessica has brought a friend!" He looked at me for help with my name.

"Frankie," I reminded him.

Fahid's reaction to seeing Jessica and me was the complete opposite to her grandfather's reaction. He ignored me and barely looked at his niece. "Shouldn't you be at school?" he asked.

"They're researching a project," Mr. Ibrahim answered for us, unfazed by his son's rudeness. Fahid moved past us into the backroom to hang up his jacket, then came back out carrying a folding chair. He positioned it directly behind Jessica. "I was just telling them about your great-great-uncle Hussein and the priest's mummy."

"Why?"

"May I?" Mr. Ibrahim asked, holding out his hand for my ankh. I lifted it over my head and gave it to him. Fahid's eyes widened at the sight of it.

"Where did you get it?" he asked.

"I don't know. I've had it since I was a child."

Fahid looked at me more intently, and his face paled. "You should go. My father and I have work to do." His voice was cold.

I was used to people reacting to me this way, but Jessica was indignant. "We're just here for a visit. We won't stay long."

Fahid shook his head. "There are things we need to discuss, and then he has a doctor's appointment."

Jessica sighed and muttered "Rude!" under her breath. We stood to go. Mr. Ibrahim passed me back my necklace. When he dropped it in my palm, he wrapped my fingers around it with his own.

"Keep it safe," he said. "Come back and visit when Fahid isn't here." He said the last part quietly, but when his eyes met mine, I knew there was more he wanted to say.

Jessica and I walked back toward school. She had to catch the bus, and I had to walk that way to get home. "Sorry about my uncle. He's a jerk."

I waved away her apology. "I'm used to it. Your grandpa's really nice, though. You're lucky."

"You don't have grandparents?" she asked.

I shrugged. "If I do, I have no idea where they are."

"You know, Frankie, you're not at all the way you look."

I snorted. "What's that supposed to mean?"

"You look kind of —" she searched for the right word "— intimidating. But you're not. I had an idea about you, but it was all wrong."

"Yeah, well, same here. I thought you were just some vapid April."

"Why do you call them 'Aprils'?"

As we walked, I told her about April Beardy. "It was easier just to not have freinds."

"She was just one person. You can't write off everyone just because she was mean to you."

I laughed. "I don't have to write them off, they write themselves off. In case you hadn't noticed, no one's begging to hang out with me."

Jessica stopped in the middle of the sidewalk and stared at me. "I literally asked you to ditch school this afternoon. I might not have begged —"

I rolled my eyes at her. "Okay, okay, I get your point."

"All I'm saying is that you should give people a chance to see the real you."

I bit back a smile, because Jessica was starting to sound a lot like Kris.

After Jessica had caught the bus, I walked home, thinking about everything I had learned from Mr. Ibrahim and how it connected to Frances and the circus. Whose soul clung to the ankh? Was it Frances's? Was that why she came to me in dreams? The only way to find out was to slip back into her world.

28

SOMETHING TERRIBLE WAS GOING TO HAPPEN, and I couldn't stop it. If I called out, Papa would realize that Gus and I had switched spots. He'd be in trouble, maybe get kicked out of the circus. I bit my lip, waiting, hoping it was just my imagination. Another gust of wind shook the canvas of the tent, and the candles still burning sputtered. I looked up. Clouds scuttled across the sky, approaching the moon with menacing speed.

Mr. Hussein's voice rose to a feverish pitch. I wanted to rush inside and pull Gus away from them, interrupt Mr. Hussein and make it stop. Yuri held one glass to Concetta's lips and one to his own. On Mr. Hussein's command, they all drank at the same time. They tipped back the glasses, choking down the liquid. Clouds covered the moon, and we were plunged into inky darkness.

There was a thud. And another and another. With wide eyes, I pushed my way into the tent and saw three bodies lying on the ground. Ahmed went down next, his wiry limbs crumpling underneath him. Elvira and Ella fell, their heads narrowly missing the sarcophagus. Mr. Hussein stared around him in wonder, as if he couldn't believe what he was witnessing.

Gus wheeled around, looking for me.

"Gus!" I rushed over to him as he began to topple.

"You must drink," he gasped, trying to pass me his glass. But he was weak, and the glass tipped over, spilling the liquid onto the ground at my feet.

"It's poison!" I screamed. "Gus!"

He fell against me, and I lost my balance. We both fell down on the ground, entangled. "Papa!" I shrieked, crying. I tried to pull myself free of Gus, but he had pinned me to the ground, the fabric of my dress caught in his stiff fingers. "Papa!"

Papa staggered to me, reaching out as if he were blind. "Frances?"

"I'm here, Papa."

"You didn't drink." It sounded as though he wanted to be angry, but didn't have the strength.

I stayed mute, horrified at the scene in front of me. "Papa!" A scream lodged itself in my throat. His face contorted in anguish.

"I can't breathe!" He clutched at his throat and made horrible gagging sounds. Falling to the ground, he stared up at me, his eyes unseeing.

Mr. Hussein was still standing at the front of the tent, surveying the scene before him with dismay. "You did this!" I shouted. "You poisoned them!"

He held up his hands. "No — I — it wasn't supposed

to happen like this …" Panicked, he was tossing everything on the table into a satchel, including what was left of the mumia powder.

"You can't leave! Help me!"

"I can't! I don't know what I did!"

He looked at the mummy behind him and then the book he'd read from. He backed away, clutching the satchel against his chest, mumbling to himself in his language.

"Where are you going?" I screamed.

"There is evil here," he gasped.

"You did this! You killed them!"

Mr. Hussein ignored me and stepped over Papa's body, clumsy in his haste.

My dress ripped as I heaved Gus off of me. I ran after Mr. Hussein, grabbing hold of his robe. "You can't leave me," I cried.

Desperation made me wild. I clawed at him, grabbing for his hands or arms, but he pushed me away and I fell to the ground. I staggered up, flung myself over Yuri, and caught Mr. Hussein's ankle, holding it tightly in my hands. He stumbled and landed on the ground beside Tabitha, now lifeless. The contents of the satchel tumbled out. His hands scrambled to collect the money that had escaped, no doubt payment for the miracle he was supposed to work.

"You killed them!" I shouted again.

Mr. Hussein kicked, trying to break free of my grip. His foot caught me in the cheek and I jerked back with a cry, letting go. Without a backward glance, he raced out of the tent and disappeared into the night. I lay on the ground, my body over Yuri's, and began to sob.

They were gone. All of them. I was alone.

Eleven bodies lay on the ground around me. Still, unmoving. I was the lone survivor. I stood on shaky legs and surveyed the tent. I was sweating and shivering, and my skin pulsed with fear.

I crawled to the glasses, hoping to scavenge enough liquid to join them. I tipped Leopold's glass to my lips. A few grainy drops leaked into my mouth. I swallowed, waiting, but felt nothing. The magic was gone.

I curled up on the ground. An ache so deep and painful that it paralyzed me. *I should have drunk.*

I moved toward Papa. His eyes were wide open and unblinking. I clung to him, laying my head on his chest, willing a heartbeat to sound. I listened, straining, but none did. He was gone. Tears came, wetting his shirt. I shook him, wailing. "Wake up! Papa!" I screamed. "Wake up!" Nothing happened. My voice disappeared like smoke into the air.

I went to Gus. His body was still warm, as if life still pulsed through him, but there was no heartbeat or breath. "Gus?" I murmured. It should have been me lying on the ground. My body ached with remorse. All he'd wanted was to stay with me. Foolish, innocent love had led to this. Just like Mama. She'd fled to protect me, and look what had happened to her.

I bent down and kissed the perfect skin on his cheek.

What would happen when the bodies were found? How could I explain what had happened? I couldn't stay, but where would I go? Abeline's words came back to me. The world would not be kind to me. Papa had intended for us to be together forever, but he'd failed. Or had he? I looked around at the entangled bodies. Maybe eternity didn't mean this life. Perhaps that was my only option — to join them in the afterlife.

Was that what I wanted?

Perhaps I should take a length of rope — but my thoughts were cut off as a gust of wind made the sides of the tent buckle and sway. A storm was on the way.

The candles that were still lit flickered. A few more sputtered out.

The wind kicked up again, the gust so violent that it ripped one rope off its stake in the ground. I screamed as the canvas fabric flapped, snapping in the air. I had to leave. I couldn't stay here. I walked to the table and picked up the lantern, surveying the bodies of the people who I cared about.

Papa wouldn't have wanted the circus to end like this. They deserved better than to be victims of a charlatan's hoax.

I swung the lantern high, and it crashed against the corner of the tent. The flame licked at the canvas and caught quickly, running up the rope and the edge of the tent flap. Flames shot up the sides, chewing through the fabric hungrily. In minutes, the whole tent was engulfed. The heat of the fire was so intense that I had to take a step back.

"Goodbye," I whispered. The fire lit up the night.

From somewhere, a scream echoed. I listened again, trying to locate the sound. Had the fire been spotted from town? Then more screams came, and they were coming from inside the tent. "Papa!" I shouted. I tried to move closer, but the fire pushed me back. It was too intense. With a thunderous crack, the poles supporting the frame crashed down, bringing the canvas with it, trapping whoever had been inside.

I moved farther back, stumbling and falling. I was sure that I had imaged the sounds. How could they be alive? There had been no heartbeats.

"Papa!" I screamed again. "Gus! Yuri!"

I couldn't hear anything over the roar of the fire. If they'd still been alive, then it wasn't the mumia powder that had killed them. It was me.

I didn't know what else to do, so I ran.

Through the bush that tore at my clothes and scratched my face, away from the roaring crackle of the tent behind me, away from the screams of the people I loved. I ran until my legs trembled with exertion and I thought I would vomit.

And then, I saw a train. Stopped on the tracks by the station.

I knew what I'd do and raced downhill towards an open side car. The train would take me away.

Its whistle pierced the air. A puff of smoke rose from its stack. The train was leaving the station. "No!" I gasped. Cries of despair rose within me. I had to get on that train. I pushed my legs to move faster, my heart beating wildly in my chest. I was close now. I could smell the rusted metal of the tracks and the coal feeding the fire.

The train's wheels started moving, slowly at first, but it would gain speed quickly. I couldn't let it leave without me. Another gust of wind rose up, pushing me, carrying me across the last stretch of land. My feet barely touched the ground as I reached out and grabbed onto a metal bar. I kicked and ran beside the train. It was moving too quickly for me to keep up. My legs failed me. I'd fall under the wheels if I let go.

A swell of air rose behind me, and I fell onto the hard planks of the train car.

I woke up exhausted and trembling. Frances had made it. She was safe.

But it was the sounds of the fire and the screaming troupe that echoed in my head. Mr. Hussein had swindled them, but it was Frances who had killed them.

29

KRIS KNOCKED ON MY DOOR and poked her head in. "Do you want coffee?" she asked. She was in her work clothes even though it was Saturday. I nodded absently. I wasn't wearing makeup, but I was too caught up with the dream and the truth of what had happened to Frances to care.

Mr. Ibrahim had told me what was needed for the mumia powder to give immortality.

They'd had the elements of earth, air, water, ether … but not fire. Not until Frances had set the tent ablaze. She'd run before discovering that the mumia powder had worked. And it must have worked, because the performers were still alive today. Hussein's spell had *worked*.

Oh my god. It seemed impossible, but I'd seen them with my own eyes.

"I'm going to the office," Kris said when she came back with a steaming mug. She cleared a place and put it on my nightstand. It was almost noon. "For a little while. I want to catch up on paperwork, and I have a meeting. I'll be a couple of hours. I'll get groceries on my way home." She hadn't yet realized that I was barely listening to her. "By the way, I talked to a digital forensics investigator about those photos," she said, sitting down on the edge of my bed. "She said hacking a phone isn't hard. All a person needs is the right software and they can get full access. View your photos, your contact list —"

Suddenly, she *did* have my attention. "Delete messages?" I asked.

Kris nodded. "You wouldn't even know the other person was there."

"Do you still think the photos are connected to your case?" I asked.

She frowned, thinking. "Why would they send *you* photos of *me*? If they wanted to scare me, it should have been the other way around."

"So maybe it is Max," I said. "Or Monsieur Duval."

"Not Max," Kris said. "It doesn't fit his profile. He's too vulnerable."

Unlike me, Kris had seen only one side of him. "He's got more edge than you'd think," I told her.

"What about Monsieur Duval?"

I shook my head. "He's so old-fashioned. I can't imagine him as a hacker." But someone had gained access to my phone and knew how important Kris was to me. And after I'd asked, *Who are you?* their response had been, *We're waiting for you*, which was eerily reminiscent of what Monsieur Duval had said to me at the warehouse show. "You'll be careful, right? Because whoever sent those pictures knows stuff about you. Where you work and what kind of car you drive."

Kris gave me a tired smile. "Don't worry about me. I can take care of myself." She glanced at my sketchbook. "More dreams?"

I snorted at the word *dreams*. "It was more like a nightmare."

Kris shifted so she could see the page better.

"Monsieur Duval had a plan to make everyone immortal. He hired this guy," I said, pointing at Hussein, "to make it happen. All the performers except Frances, drank mumia powder. A ground-up Egyptian mummy," I explained.

"And they all died?" Kris asked, looking at the picture of them lying on the ground.

"Frances thought the mumia powder had killed them. Since she couldn't bury them, she set fire to the tent and then she heard them screaming."

"They weren't dead?" Kris's eyes widened.

I shook my head. "They got trapped in the tent."

"Frankie, that's a terrible dream!"

The performers' screams echoed in my head. "She ran away." I turned to the last page. It was a rough sketch of Frances sitting in a boxcar. "Can you imagine what it was like thinking she'd caused their deaths? She was only ten."

"And the performers, these are the people you saw at Comicon and at the warehouse?"

"They found the secret to eternal life," I said. "In my dream, anyway."

I would have thought it sounded impossible, too, so I didn't blame Kris for the look of disbelief she gave me. "The only one who's not still with them is Frances."

Kris flipped through my drawings again. She paused at one of the final ones, where the tent was on fire. "You were ten when we found you."

That had been the best guess, anyway. Kris looked at me like I should be connecting the dots. "Maybe we've been looking at this all wrong. Maybe the circus you're dreaming about represents your family? You've invented a make-believe life in your subconscious that mirrors what really happened to you."

"You think I killed my family?" I looked at her, horrified.

"No!" she said, adamantly. "But there could have been a fire. And then you ran like Frances did. You could have survivor's guilt."

I squeezed my eyes shut and saw the tent engulfed in flames. Or was it a house in the middle of a field?

Whose screams echoed in my head? The performers' or my family's? Frances's pain had been so real to me. In my heart, I knew what guilt like hers felt like.

How would I know that unless I'd set the fire?

Kris's phone rang. She peeked at the number and her face fell. "That's my client," she said. I wished she'd let it go to voice mail, but I knew she couldn't do that. "Hang on," she said to me and answered the phone. "Hello?" Client phone calls were rarely short. They only called when there was a crisis. Kris looked at me helplessly and moved into the hallway to continue the call in private.

I flipped back a few pages in my sketchbook and studied the drawing I'd done of Monsieur Duval consoling Frances in her tent. Monsieur Duval had loved Frances. So had Gus.

I squeezed my eyes shut. Keeping what I knew in this world and what I'd seen in my dreams straight was giving me a headache. And now Kris has planted the idea that the dreams weren't of the circus, but of my past.

A hundred years ago, Frances had run from the circus thinking the performers were dead. In the present, I'd met almost all of them. The only ones missing were Frances and Gus.

I pulled the laptop onto my bed and scrolled through the photos I'd bookmarked until I came to the one of the whole troupe. I zoomed in on Gus's face. Up close, it was grainy, but I cropped it and copied it, then opened a document in Photoshop. I gave him short hair, bleached it out, and added glasses. His eye colour went from green to brown. I wasn't totally surprised when the face looking back at me wasn't Gus. It was Max.

I'd been thinking it was Monsieur Duval trying to lure me back to the circus with the Comicon and warehouse shows, but it hadn't been just him. Max had been in on this, too. But why? What did they want? And why send the stalkerazzi photos of Kris? What were they trying to prove?

I slumped against my headboard. Trying to make sense of it myself was only making my headache worse, but I needed answers.

Kris was still on the phone when I emerged from my room. I hadn't spent as much time as usual getting ready. Except for foundation, my makeup was minimal, and I'd thrown on a black hoodie and jeans. The ankh felt heavy around my neck. I had my pocket knife, too.

"Where are you going?" Kris mouthed. She pointed to the phone and grimaced.

I grabbed a notepad and wrote *flea market*. So far, the only person who'd been able to give me answers about the circus and the mumia powder was Mr. Ibrahim. Maybe he'd also be able to explain how I was connected.

Kris took the pen from me. *Okay. Sorry! We'll talk when I get back.*

My phone was lying on the counter. Kris glanced at it and shook her head, a silent message to leave it behind. If someone was controlling it remotely, they could use it to track me. Right now, the less the circus had to do with me, the better.

When I got to Mr. Ibrahim's booth at the flea market, he wasn't at his desk.

"Mr. Ibrahim?" I called.

"He's in the back," the lady across the aisle said. "Probably making some tea. Just go on in. He won't mind." I looked at her doubtfully and called for him one more time. When he didn't answer, I went behind his desk and peeked on the other side of the partition.

He was sitting on the floor at a low table. Another man was with him, but his back was to me. "Sorry to bother you, Mr. Ibrahim. The lady across the way said to come back here."

Mr. Ibrahim grinned at me. "Frankie! We were just talking about you."

The other man turned around. "Hello, Frankie." It was Monsieur Duval. My breath caught in my throat.

"What are you doing here?" I managed to splutter. I didn't have my phone. He couldn't have tracked me.

"Tomar and I are old friends. I knew his great-uncle."

"Hussein," I said.

Monsieur Duval nodded. "You look so worried," he said sadly. "I promise, you have nothing to fear from me."

After my dream last night and the business with my phone, I wasn't so sure. "How did you know I'd be here?"

"Truly, it's a coincidence. I'm here to visit Tomar. We often have tea together when I'm in town."

I looked at Jessica's grandfather. Was he one of them? I stayed by the entrance, wary of getting any closer. "I saw Frances's memory of the night you drank the mumia powder."

I knew it was the fire she set that had given them immortality, but did he? Monsieur Duval paused. If he truly was over a hundred years old, in that moment, he looked it.

"Yes, we owe our everlasting lives to Frances," he said quietly. "Little did she know the consequences of her actions."

Mr. Ibrahim put his elbows on the table and clasped his hands together. "Philippe has a lot to tell you, Frankie. Perhaps you should sit."

The woman across the aisle had seen me come to Mr. Ibrahim's booth, and I'd told Kris where I was going. Had Monsieur Duval been watching Kris? Was he the one who'd sent the photos? Was I safe?

Monsieur Duval read my hesitation. "I make you uncomfortable," he said.

"I don't understand how we're connected. What is it about me?"

He gave me a weary smile. "I can explain everything, I promise. But please, sit."

Mr. Ibrahim nodded. "You're my granddaughter's friend. I wouldn't let anything happen to you." He held up the long-necked copper teapot that was sitting in the middle of the table. "But first, tea."

The liquid came out in a long stream over mashed-up mint and teaspoons of sugar sitting at the bottom of the glasses. The aroma was sweet and fresh.

Both Mr. Ibrahim and Monsieur Duval reached for their glasses. I hesitated for just a moment, then took mine. The tea didn't taste like tea at all. It was thick and syrupy and slid down my throat like honey.

"I know you have many questions. Will you indulge me, Frankie, as I tell you about the years since that fateful night?" His words were like honey, too. Sweet and tempting. He was the fatherly Monsieur Duval from Frances's childhood. I nodded, and he began speaking.

"I am embarrassed to admit that despite my long life, I am not an educated man. While I frittered away my years with more creative pursuits and travel, Yuri pursued education. That man studied at every major university and has an alphabet of degrees after his name. He obtained a medical degree from Harvard University many years ago, and that is where our story begins."

He paused to sip his tea. "I tell you this because as a doctor, he was privy to medical records, which allowed him to fulfill my request. I asked him to tell me if he ever came across a marvel similar to my beloved Frances."

"He agreed, probably thinking it was nothing more than one of my eccentricities. As you know, your condition is rare. I just had to give it time," he said with a wry smile. "Luckily, I have a lot of that. What good fortune it was when Yuri told me that he had found a little girl, a potential Frances. I'm sure you can guess who she was."

"Me."

He nodded. "I kept you a secret for a long time. But as you grew, I wondered what would happen. The world was changing. What I'd called marvels were being given much crueller names."

I thought about how Frances had felt the day she'd run from the stage. The boys' repulsion had been too much for her. "I know it is for this reason that you hide your skin under makeup." The depth of his gaze made me avert my eyes.

"All of the performers found ways to while away the years. Gus chose to spend his time a different way." He paused. "The boy Gus from the circus is —"

"Max," I finished.

Monsieur Duval nodded. "He wasn't sure how long the bleached hair and glasses would fool you." He gave me a grim smile and continued. "Gus taught himself all that he could learn about computers. He's become very proficient. Without Yuri's help, he learned of your existence when you were nine years old by hacking into a database of medical records."

I let this sink in. "He's the one who messed with my phone."

"Among other things."

"He misses Frances terribly. He blames himself for what happened. If he hadn't switched spots with her, Frances would be where she belongs. With us." There was an edge to his voice, as if Gus was getting what he deserved. "Without my knowledge, he sought you out and befriended you while you were young." A chill went up my spine. That explained why he seemed familiar. "He attended your school and spent time with your family."

My family. The idea that Gus had memories of them when I didn't turned my stomach.

"He claimed that they mistreated you and that we should save you from them. There was no proof of this. I think Gus made it up to convince us to do what he wanted."

"Which was what?" I asked.

"To have you join us."

I stared at Monsieur Duval.

"I said no. You were too young, and by then I'd realized that replacing Frances was impossible. Our days as the Circus of Marvels and Wonders have been over for a long time."

I looked at him suspiciously. "That's not what you said at the warehouse."

A benevolent look crossed his face, like the look a grandfather would give his favourite grandchild. "I didn't think there was any harm in trying. I doubted you'd agree, but Gus was insistent. He thought maybe we could entice you."

"So Max — er, Gus was behind all of this?" At these words, Monsieur Duval bent his head and nodded.

"And my family?"

"There was a fire," he said quietly.

The sound of screams and crashing timbers echoed in my head. A flash of heat, and then I was running. I gasped. The memory was there, dancing around my consciousness.

"Gus underestimated how much losing your family would traumatize you. He was in over his head, and he had no idea how to help you. You were inconsolable. It was horrible to see a child in so much pain — not physical, but emotional. Just as I had warned him, taking you at such a young age was a mistake. He kept you for a few weeks, trying to care for you. At one point, you fought so viciously, you fell and hit your head. Gus called me in a panic. He thought you were dead."

"The concussion." My fingers strayed to the scar at my hairline. "Why didn't he get me to drink the mumia powder then?" I asked.

"A few reasons," Monsieur Duval said. "He wanted you to be closer to his age, for one thing. And he needed to find someone who could perform the ceremony. Hussein was long dead by then. The other missing piece was ether. You had to *want* to be changed. He thought if you, as an orphan, grew to love us, you'd want to join us."

Monsieur Duval continued. "When you came to, we could tell you had a serious concussion. You didn't seem to remember a thing about any of us, or your life before us. We asked Yuri for help. He was disgusted at what Gus had done. He said you needed proper care at a hospital, but a hospital would ask questions. He had no medical records, no identity documents for you. He'd started calling you Frances by then. It was Gus who spotted the police cruiser from the warehouse window. He put you in an alley where he knew you'd be found. Your amnesia worked in our favour, I'm sorry to say."

"Oh my god," I murmured. My head throbbed. When I closed my eyes, I saw the blinding glare of the police car headlights shining in the alley. I'd tried to run, scrambling over bags of garbage, terrified as they came closer.

Monsieur Duval's voice was strained when he started to speak again. "I watched as you were taken away. I made Gus swear he would not come after you again. But he didn't listen, and that's why he's back."

"Nothing has changed, though," I said. "I still don't want to join you!"

Monsieur Duval sighed. "As I said, he's insistent that you can be convinced."

"How?"

"I'm not sure. He and I are at odds. He doesn't trust me like he used to."

"What about the other performers? They're going along with his plans?"

A worn-out look passed over Monsieur Duval's face. "I wish I could explain what eternity feels like. It's being trapped and set free at the same time. We're bound to each other in a way no mortal could understand. Lifetimes mean nothing when forever stretches out in front of us. It's changed who we are and what we're willing to do. There's no escape from ourselves." He leaned in and whispered, "I would welcome death."

"Are you afraid of Gus?" I asked.

"Me? No, but I'm afraid of what he'll do to get Frances back."

"Get her back how? Is she still alive?"

Monsieur Duval shook his head. He glanced at Mr. Ibrahim, who nodded for him to continue. "We have her soul."

"Her soul?" I repeated.

"Hussein didn't get far the night of the fire. Word spread that there had been a fire, but that the performers were alive and well. Of course, he had to come back to see for himself."

Mr. Ibrahim picked up the story, "As a child, my great-uncle told me stories. I always thought they were made up. Fantasy stories for his favourite grandnephew. My favourite tale was about a girl whose soul had been trapped in an ankh. Like the legends of genies trapped in bottles, her soul would remain there until it was freed."

Monsieur Duval, composed again, continued speaking. "The night Frances died, Hussein pulled out the *Book of the Dead*. He muttered and did incantations while we stood beside him, still shocked at what we had become. When the sun rose, Gus swore he saw Frances's soul drift out of her body and into the ankh."

I pulled the ankh out from under my hoodie and looked down at it. "Her soul is in here?" As impossible as it sounded, I knew it wasn't. After all, I was sitting across from someone who should have died years ago.

"That's what Gus believes."

"But not you?"

Monsieur Duval thought for a moment before continuing. "Whether it is or not, I've learned that it's not our place to meddle with things that we don't understand. I've learned my lesson," he said with a sigh. "Gus, on the other hand, holds out hope that he will be reunited with her."

"If he's right about her soul, that would explain why her memories have been coming to me."

Mr. Ibrahim nodded. "I told you, it's dark magic." He lifted his sleeve and revealed the same tattoo as Monsieur Duval's and Max's. "One that my great-uncle brought into this world, and one that he charged me to protect." He exchanged a rueful smile with Monsieur Duval. "My family is bound to them, our punishment for unleashing the curse."

"Your family," I said. "Does that mean —"

"Jessica is my only grandchild. One day she will carry this burden. She will be tattooed as I am, and as Gus, Monsieur Duval, and the other performers are."

The thought of Jessica being mixed up with Gus made my chest ache.

I picked up the ankh and let it rest on my palm. "Why would he give it to me if he thought it was so special? I could have lost it, or it might have been taken away from me." And then Frances's soul would have been lost.

"He didn't give it to you — I did," Monsieur Duval said. "Gus didn't know until you'd been taken away. Of course, he was furious with me, but I told him that Frances would watch over you. When you were old enough, if you wanted to discover your past, the ankh would lead you to us. To be honest, I never expected it to happen. I thought over the years that Gus's dream would die."

"But it didn't," I said angrily.

"There's more." Monsieur Duval shook his head and sighed. "Gus was in your house, Frankie. About two weeks ago, he broke in, looking for the ankh. He's planning something. Something to do with you."

I hated thinking about Gus in Kris's house, rifling through our things. He'd probably found my sketchbook and maybe my school schedule, and who knew what else? "That was the first night I dreamed about you," I remembered.

Mr. Ibrahim and Monsieur Duval exchanged a look. I could tell they had something to tell me, but neither one wanted to.

"What is it?"

"He's found a way to put her soul into your body."

I gulped. "How?"

Monsieur Duval held his hands out helplessly. "He won't tell me. All I know is that it's going to happen tonight. There's a full moon, just as there was the night of our ceremony."

"But Hussein's been dead for years, right? There's no one to perform the ceremony." For a moment, I felt a flicker of optimism.

Mr. Ibrahim shook his head. "I told you, my family is bound to the circus. That bond extends to my son, Fahid."

I remembered the chilly greeting I'd gotten yesterday. It had nothing to do with my gothness. "He's working with Gus?"

"We think so. Fahid has studied the *Book of the Dead*. He knows it as well as I do. He might be capable of performing the ceremony to free Frances's soul and put it into your immortal body. He's bold enough to try."

The words *immortal* and *soul* swirled in my head. "But I don't want to join you," I said looking at Monsieur Duval and then back to Mr. Ibrahim. "The other day, you said ether was an essential part of the spell. It won't work if I don't want to be changed, right?"

Mr. Ibrahim sighed. Loose skin sagged under his eyes. "He'll try to convince you."

"How?"

"This is what we've been trying to figure out. What could he say or do that would push you to go along with him?" They both looked at me.

He knew where I went to school, and that I was good at art. And he knew I lived with Kris. A shiver of dread ran along my spine.

Across the table, I met Monsieur Duval's eyes. "There's only one person in my life that I care about enough to save. He's going to go after my foster mom." I cursed myself for ever having told him anything. For letting him into my life. I ran through the few times Gus and I had been together, trying to untangle them. From the first moment when he'd met me at school, he'd been reeling me in, bit by bit.

The argument after school and his weird behaviour made more sense now. Instead of growing closer to him, I'd pulled away. And now Kris's life was in danger. Threatening her was the only way to get me to agree to his insane plan.

My skin went clammy, itching under my makeup. I didn't have my phone. "I need to call her," I said, panic straining my voice. As Mr. Ibrahim pulled a phone out of his pocket, he looked at Monsieur Duval. "There is a way to stop him."

"Yes," Monsieur Duval agreed. "But it would mean an end to everything."

I looked between them. "Whatever it is, we have to do it. We have to save Kris."

They both nodded . "Very well. But before you make the call," Mr. Ibrahim said gently, "you must listen. Kris's life depends on it."

I tried to calm my heartbeat and focus on what he said. As they laid out their plan, I saw just how dangerous Gus was.

30

*P*LEASE ANSWER, I prayed as I dialed Kris's number and held the phone to my ear.

"Hello? This is Kris Steffanson."

I let out a sigh of relief when I heard her voice. "It's me." She wouldn't recognize Mr. Ibrahim's number. "I had to borrow someone's phone," I quickly explained. "Where are you?"

"In my car. I got a call from the trauma unit about an active situation. I'm on my way there now. It might just be a coincidence, but —"

"What? What is it? Where are you going?" I asked. I was already out of the flea market and walking across the parking lot with Mr. Ibrahim's phone glued to my ear. He and Monsieur Duval would be leaving a few minutes after me. I raised my arm to signal for a cab. As soon as one pulled over, I jumped in.

Kris hesitated. Her professional code of conduct would be compromised if she told me too much. "The same warehouse you went to last weekend, on Mitchell Avenue."

"Kris, listen to me ..." But there was no time to explain it all. She wouldn't have believed me even if I did. A taxi pulled up. A lady got out, and before she could close the door, I grabbed it and slid into the backseat. "I'm in a cab. I'll be there soon," I told her. "Don't do anything until I get there."

"This is an active situation," she said, confused. "You won't be allowed in. I shouldn't have told you where I was going."

"Please, listen to me. It's not safe —"

"I'm not going in alone. I'll have backup. I've got to go. I'm almost there." The next thing I knew, she was gone.

The crowded sidewalks started to empty the closer the taxi got to Mitchell Avenue. "Can't you go any faster?" I asked the driver. My foot tapped impatiently. If anything, my question made him drive slower.

"You've got money to pay me, right?" he asked. The money Jessica had given me was in my bag. I pulled the bills out and waved them.

"Yes. Just hurry, okay?"

When the cab pulled to a stop in front of the chain-link fence that surrounded the warehouse, I tossed a twenty onto the passenger's seat and got out of the car.

"You want your change?" the driver shouted out the window. I shook my head and heard the car accelerate as he drove away.

The warehouse loomed ahead of me. It looked different in the daylight, grungier and more dilapidated than I remembered. I still had a knot of fear in my gut. I didn't know what was waiting inside for me. Kris's car was parked to the left of the building, but she wasn't inside it. There weren't any other cars around. If what Monsieur Duval said was true, Gus had probably faked the call, and he could have hacked into the police scanners and rerouted backup if it had been called for. At this point, I wasn't putting anything past him.

"Kris!" I shouted. No answer. I wondered if he was watching me, enjoying the drama of my approach. A door on the main floor was ajar, so I went toward it, but I knew there was no way Kris would have gone into the building alone. I couldn't watch detective shows with her because she'd mutter over the inaccuracies. The thing that bugged her the most was when a cop didn't wait for backup. "That's so unrealistic," she'd moan. If she'd gone inside the warehouse, it hadn't been by choice. Kris might have been trained in self-defence, but she'd be no match for Thor.

I didn't bother shouting for her. Using my foot, I nudged the door open and stepped inside. The main floor was huge, dim, and empty. Another door on the left led to a dark, windowless stairwell. I turned on the flashlight on Mr. Ibrahim's phone and went up the stairs, pausing on the second-floor landing. I saw a makeshift living space, but no sign of Kris or Gus. Whatever he had planned was waiting for me on the third floor. I kept climbing.

At the top of the next set of stairs was a velvet curtain. "Gus?" My voice was reed thin with nerves. There was no answer. I fumbled with the heavy fabric until I found an opening. When I stepped through, I found myself on a stage. The only light came from clusters of candles that gave the space a spooky glow. Kris was in the middle of the stage, her arms and legs tied to a chair, duct tape over her mouth.

Her eyes flashed with terror when she saw me. I froze where I was. Gus stepped out from the other side of the stage. He looked less like Max and more like the boy from my dreams. He walked with confidence, his previous wariness gone. It had never been real. Without his glasses, wearing a T-shirt and jeans, and with Monsieur Duval's top hat and silver-tipped walking stick, he was in control. Gus was the ringmaster now.

I looked to my right. In a row of chairs set up in front of the stage sat some of the performers. Ahmed had a pained look on his face and wouldn't meet my eyes. Ella and Elvira shared a chair, their usually perky red lips pale and drawn. Yuri wouldn't look at me, either, and Daniel's hair was matted and dirty. Leopold gulped when my eyes landed on him.

I swallowed back the fear that rose in my throat and turned to Gus. "Finally," he breathed, taking a few steps closer. "You've come. I've waited so long for you to join us."

"Let Kris go."

"I will," he agreed, then gave a little laugh, clearly enjoying his time on the stage. All eyes were on him. He circled Kris slowly, like a predator. "You could have made it easier for us, you know. Monsieur Duval tried to tell you what we wanted the last time you were here." He waited for me to stay something.

"I got scared," I stammered.

He gave me a disarming smile, as if he were trying to put me at ease. It did the opposite. "There's nothing to be scared of. We don't want to hurt you. Joining us will be the best thing you've ever done. I have so many plans for what we can do with the circus."

So many plans. I'd heard that before. From Boyfriend #3. He saw me as something to be exploited. *I have so many plans,* he'd said, and then locked the door behind him. When I looked at Gus, I saw the same hunger, and it turned my stomach.

Had Frances seen it, too, when he'd laid out his plans for the circus?

When I'd been trapped with Boyfriend #3, I'd been scared and too ashamed to do anything about it. But this time, knowing what Gus had in store for me, the fear didn't make me cower; it lit a spark. The rage that had festered in me for years, that had lashed out at Kris and anyone who'd tried to help me, flickered to life. As long as I controlled it, I could use it. Gus thought he had all the power, but he didn't know what I was capable of. Before I'd left the flea market stall, Monsieur Duval had asked if my love for Kris was stronger than my fear of Gus.

There'd been no hesitation in my answer.

"I've had lots of time to think," Gus continued. "The sky is the limit to what I can do. What *we* can do!" His voice had the volume and cadence of a showman, just like Monsieur Duval in my dreams. I glanced at the curtains, hoping for movement. Monsieur Duval and Mr. Ibrahim should have been here by now.

Gus waved the walking stick at the assembled audience. "We will be reborn as the Immortal Circus! It will be the stuff of dreams! Exclusive to the wealthiest people. Imagine the thrill of dining at a table full of immortals! It'll be like dining with the gods!"

He dropped the voice and came closer to me. "I want you by my side. You will be the star of the show. I've already thought of your stage name. Are you ready?" He looked at me, a smile bursting across his face. "You won't be Alligator Girl anymore. Your new name will be —" there was a dramatic pause "— Serpentina the Reptilian Queen."

I looked at him with disgust. "I won't be your anything," I spat.

From the audience, Ella and Elvira shook their heads, tsking my rudeness. Leopold shifted uncomfortably.

Gus's face fell, as if he was annoyed I wasn't playing along with his charade. "That's true, actually. It won't be you who travels around the world with me. Your body, but not your soul."

I kept my gaze level and met his eyes. "Frances doesn't want to join you."

He laughed. "Yes, she does. Of course, she does!"

I shook my head. "I saw what happened the night of the fire. She left you and never looked back."

His voice turned angry. "That's not true! The night of the fire, she wanted to come back to us."

"No. I've seen her memories. She jumped on a train to be free."

"Freedom is what we have. Immortality. We're not chained to this world by a fear of death. Are we?" He turned to the performers. A few shook their heads. "If Frances had known the gift she'd given us, she'd have stayed."

"I don't believe you," I said. "I think you want her back because she's the one person you haven't found a way to control."

"I loved her." He narrowed his eyes, considering me. "You don't know everything that happened that night."

"Tell her," Ella said from the audience.

"Yes, I want to hear it again," Elvira agreed.

"Fine." He took a breath and began to speak. His voice had a faraway quality to it, as if he'd told the story many times before. "When I woke up, the tent was on fire. I was terrified. I started screaming, looking for a way out through the flames. A piece of fabric fell on me. But instead of lighting me on fire, it slid off, as though I were made of stone. The others started to wake up, too. None of us was injured, not even with a fire raging around us." The performers murmured amongst themselves. A hundred years later, the memory of the fire still made them uncomfortable.

"I looked for Frances and saw the empty goblet on the ground. I cried out for her, but there was no answer. I ran to the top of the hill. In the moonlight, I saw her racing across the field toward the train."

As he spoke, Frances's dream came back to me. I remembered the relief she'd felt as she scrambled onto the train and clung to the side of the boxcar.

"I sprinted down the hill, yelling her name, but the train was too loud. It was still moving slowly, but once it left the station and picked up speed, I'd have no chance of catching it. I ran, shouting, 'Frances! Frances!'

"Finally, as I got closer, she heard me and looked out from a boxcar. Her white dress glowed in the moonlight. She shone like an angel. 'Gus!' she screamed.

"'Jump!' I shouted. 'I'll catch you!' The train was going faster. Frances stretched out a hand to me. Our fingertips nearly touched. 'Now!' I yelled. She jumped, as far from the tracks as she could, but her dress caught on something. She hung there, suspended over the tracks like a helpless rag doll. I pumped my arms and legs, running as fast as I could to catch her and pull her to safety."

I waited with bated breath. Monsieur Duval had told me she'd died, but I'd never asked how or when. Had it been that night?

"Her dress began to rip. Inch by inch, and then all at once. She fell and disappeared under the wheels." Remorse made his voice thick. All the performers sat in tearful silence as he recounted Frances's final moments. Ella and Elvira dabbed at their eyes. Daniel bowed his head.

"She died on the tracks on the same night she was supposed to live forever."

"But the ankh!" Ella piped up. "She was wearing the ankh!"

"Yes, the ankh." His eyes drifted back to me. "It was luck, or maybe fate, that she was wearing it when she died."

"What happened?" I asked.

"Her body was mangled. I —" he broke off, wincing. "I picked her up and carried her back."

"We sat with her," Ella piped up.

Gus nodded. "And then Hussein came back."

"Townspeople had seen the flames and come to check on us. Philippe assured them we were fine. When word spread —" Leopold began.

"And Hussein heard. He had to know if it was true." Elvira finished.

"There was another ceremony, held in the smouldering ashes of our circus," Yuri sighed. "As dawn broke."

"It worked. We all saw it," Ella said.

"Saw what?" I asked.

"A silvery thread hovering over her body. Her soul," Leopold murmured.

Gus nodded. "It floated over to the ankh and disappeared inside." He looked at me with eyes full of wonder. "It was magic. For just a second, the ankh glowed, and I knew Frances wasn't gone. She was still with us."

He turned to the performers. "And after tonight, she'll be with us again."

No one moved, not onstage or in the audience.

Was joining them what Frances wanted? In my dreams, she'd tried to escape the circus. If Gus had his way, she'd be bound to them for eternity. A showpiece. A freak to be ogled by the highest bidders. I couldn't let that happen. I knew why she'd shown me her memories. It wasn't just to protect me, it was so I could save her.

Gus spun around. "It's time to get on with the ceremony." He was back in showman mode, commanding the stage. He tapped the walking stick on the stage three times. "Mr. Ibrahim," he called. My heart stopped. *Mr. Ibrahim?* He was working with me, not Gus. Or was he? Had everything at the flea market been part of some bigger plan to fool me into trusting him? With a dramatic flourish, Gus stood aside as the curtains parted, and I nearly fainted with relief. It wasn't Jessica's grandfather, but her uncle who stepped onto the stage.

"What are you doing?" I asked him. The tremble in my voice wasn't totally fake. I'd thought Monsieur Duval and the other Mr. Ibrahim would be here by now. Or were they hiding out of sight until Fahid took the stage?

In his white robe, Fahid's resemblance to Mr. Hussein was striking. "Claiming my birthright," he said.

"Fahid will make an excellent addition to our show, selling immortality to others. How much would someone pay to live forever? What do you think? Ten million dollars? A hundred million?"

"You have to prove he can do it first," I pointed out. I was doing my best not to let him see how shaken I was.

"And if he can't do it," a voice called from behind the curtains, "I have a backup plan." From the same side of the stage I'd entered from, Monsieur Duval appeared with Mr. Ibrahim, just as we'd planned. The old man's hands were bound behind his back. "Tomar knows as much about the spells as Fahid does."

There was a moment of shocked silence as the audience took in the scene on the stage. Even Gus looked surprised. Fahid stared at his father, bewildered.

"Monsieur Duval!" Ella and Elvira clapped at his entrance. He gave a small bow, nodding to the others as well.

"I wondered where you'd gone," Gus said. "If you're back, does it mean you've changed your mind? You're willing to go along with the plan?"

I noticed the way Monsieur Duval's eyes narrowed at the sight of his top hat and walking stick. "Yes, I've reconsidered," he said. "Is that my top hat?"

Gus gave him a condescending smile. "It looks good on me, doesn't it?"

A veiled look came over Monsieur Duval's face. I wondered if it was taking every bit of his energy not to lunge across the stage and take back his hat and walking stick.

Mr. Ibrahim tried to shirk away from Monsieur Duval. "I won't help you," he said through clenched teeth. "And you," he seethed, glaring at Fahid, "have betrayed our family!"

"Careful, Tomar." Monsieur Duval tightened his grip and Tomar winced. "Remember, your granddaughter's life is at stake."

Mr. Ibrahim gasped. He was playing his role perfectly.

Gus turned to me, pointing the walking stick in my direction. "Now, Frankie. Are you ready?" His face glowed with anxious excitement. He'd waited a long time for this moment.

Throughout all of the action on stage, Kris had sat quietly, watching. But now, she shook her head wildly, trying to get my attention. She struggled to make sounds through the tape over her mouth. I made a move toward her, but Gus held up the walking stick and blocked me. "Remember," he said, "if you don't drink the mumia, or if the plan doesn't work, she dies."

My life and Kris's were on the line. I'd put all my faith in the plan Monsieur Duval and Mr. Ibrahim had designed. All I could do was hope it worked. "I have to do it, Kris. I don't have a choice. I can't let them hurt you."

Gus motioned for Daniel and Yuri to move a tall rectangular table to the stage and place it in front of Fahid. It was covered in a white tablecloth. Next, Leopold carried over a tray with a pitcher of water and a glass on it. A small crystal bowl held what looked to be ashes, but I knew it was something more sinister. Beside that was a bowl of soil. *Earth, air, water, ether, and* — my throat tightened at the thought of the fifth element — *fire*. Yuri took the tray from Leopold and put it on the table. When the stage was set, they all went back to their chairs.

"Let Kris go." My voice shook.

"I will, after the ceremony has been completed. I need to trust you'll do your part."

Behind the table, Fahid cleared his throat. "Can we begin?"

Gus looked at the table with satisfaction, as if he were checking off a mental to-do list. "We have everything," he said. "Well, almost everything." He turned to

Ahmed and handed him a book of matches. "As soon as she drinks, go downstairs and help Thor start the fire." He turned to me and held out his hand. "The ankh," he said. "You can give it to me by choice, or I can take it by force."

I lifted the ankh over my head and said a silent good-bye to Frances. For a fraction of a second, I glanced at Monsieur Duval, but his eyes were trained on Gus. Gus brought the ankh to his lips, whispered something, and put it on the table in front of Fahid.

Kris made noises and stamped her feet, trying to get my attention. Tears ran down her cheeks. She was ter-rified for me.

"Remember why you're doing this," Gus said. He pointed the walking stick at Kris. "You *want* the spell to work, because it means she lives." He moved closer and pressed the tip into Kris's chest. She looked at me, shaking her head. *Don't do it*, her eyes said.

"Let us begin." Fahid raised his arms up to the sky and began to chant. His voice rose, gaining speed and volume as the prayer took hold.

I watched, breathless, as Gus poured water into the glass and then, with magician-like flair, scooped spoon-fuls of the mumia powder into it. The water turned cloudy. He walked toward me with the glass. Kris banged her feet on the ground, snorting and moaning. *It's no use*, I wanted to tell her. *Even if you were able to get free, we wouldn't be able to escape them. Not yet.*

Gus brought the glass to my lips. From the corner of my eye, I saw Monsieur Duval watching me, urging me to take a sip. In their chairs, the performers leaned forward. I fought the impulse to whack the glass out of Gus's hands. *Don't lose control*, I reminded myself.

Not now. Monsieur Duval nodded at me. Fahid's voice reached a crescendo.

Kris's screams were muffled as she rocked the chair so violently, it tipped over. And then she was silent. I closed my eyes and let the liquid slide down my throat.

31

JUST AS THE PERFORMERS HAD DONE in my dream, I
dropped to the floor and lay there, waiting. Mr. Ibrahim
had assured me that while the performers had lay dead for
some time before they'd been reborn by the fire, the same
thing wouldn't happen this time. According to Mr. Ibrahim,
Hussein was the original desecrator of the mummy, so the
power of the priest's curse ended when Hussein died. I
hoped Mr. Ibrahim had been telling the truth.

"She drank!" Gus shouted. "Start the fire!"

I heard footsteps and chairs toppling over. "I still
hate fire," Ella said. "Get me out of here."

"I'm going as fast as I can," said her twin.

"I'd like to stay and watch." This was Yuri. I imagined him peering at me, his scientific mind curious to
see what happened next.

"No," Gus said. "You need to leave. Someone might
call 911, and then we'll have to explain what we're doing here." Yuri sighed but didn't argue. There was a

flurry of activity as the performers left. Now I understood why Concetta, Tabitha, and Shirley were missing. They wouldn't have been able to move fast enough.

"Did it work?" Fahid asked.

"We'll see," said Gus. Droplets of water fell on my face and clothes. And then, handfuls of dirt. "We'll know once the fire comes. It was the fire that breathed life into us. Go now, Fahid. I'll be out soon."

"Put the ankh beside her," Fahid said. "Her first breath as an immortal will pull the soul into her body. That is how the spell works."

I kept my eyes glued shut as the ankh was placed on the floor in front of me. If Gus had checked for my heartbeat, he would have felt it hammering in my chest. But even so, he wouldn't have known whether that was normal or not. Frances was the only one who'd seen what had happened that night.

"Philippe, aren't you coming?" Yuri called to Monsieur Duval.

"No, I'll stay with Frankie. Look after the others?"

"Of course," Yuri said solemnly.

"I'm the only one who is going to stay with her. That's what we agreed on," Gus said.

"I am still the head of this circus, even if you are wearing my top hat and carrying my walking stick." Monsieur Duval's voice was like acid. He couldn't hide his feelings toward Gus any longer.

"About that," Gus said. I could hear how he savoured his next words, as if he'd been waiting a long time to say them and didn't want to rush it. "The circus is no longer in need of your services."

Monsieur Duval spluttered. "No longer — what are you playing at, Gus? Don't you remember who you are?"

"I do. Very well. It's you who forgets who I am. I found Frankie. I brought her to us. I found Fahid. Soon I'll have Frances back, as well. I don't want Frances to be torn between us. Her loyalty should be with me. Which is why your time has come, Monsieur Duval."

I could smell smoke. Thor and Ahmed had started the fire beneath us.

"Have you forgotten I'm immortal?" Monsieur Duval asked with a snort. "That knife can't kill me."

Knife? I couldn't keep my eyes closed any longer. They flew open. Gus's back was to me. He was advancing toward Monsieur Duval.

"This knife can."

Wisps of smoke floated up from the staircase. I needed to make a move. The ankh lay on the ground in front of me. Cautiously, I inched my fingers toward it and then pulled it back to me and stuffed it into my pocket, pulling out *my* knife. A few feet away, Kris was also on the ground. Her eyes were closed and a new wave of panic hit me. Was she okay? She was still breathing, but she must have hit her head when she fell. Gus hadn't turned around. He was focused on Monsieur Duval, moving closer to him and farther from me. Crawling on my belly, I went to Kris. I needed to get her out of here.

"How can that knife kill me?" Monsieur Duval asked.

"Fahid has taught me a lot. Most importantly, that only the person who casts the spell can break it."

"That makes no sense. Hussein is dead. Has been for years."

"But his great-grandnephew isn't! Fahid has enough of Hussein's blood in his veins that a knife dipped in it will turn you to dust. That's his blood on the blade."

Was that possible? I looked at Mr. Ibrahim. His eyes were wide with surprise. I had a choice to make: escape with Kris, or do something to save Duval.

Clouds of smoke billowed up from below. The fire was spreading. The smell triggered a memory. A house ... in a field, or was it a tent? Was I remembering my past, or Frances's?

Kris coughed and I shook off the memory. I looked at Mr. Ibrahim again. He was mouthing something. "My blood." *Of course!* Fahid wasn't the only one with Hussein's blood flowing through his veins.

I crawled to Mr. Ibrahim and cut the ropes off his wrists. He held his palm flat, and I sliced the knife cleanly across it. Bright-red blood dripped onto the stage and coated my knife.

Smoke spilled out of the doorway. The staircase was no longer safe for him. He'd have to use the fire escape on the outside of the building. Monsieur Duval had done a good job distracting Gus. They were deep in an argument about who was fit to lead the circus. Gus hadn't noticed what was going on behind him. "The fire escape," I whispered and nodded in its direction. "It's down that hallway."

As soon as Mr. Ibrahim stood up and began to run, Gus turned, but kept his knife pointed at Monsieur Duval. His eyes narrowed in anger when he saw me, alive and well. "Why didn't it work!"

Monsieur Duval laughed. "Curses are funny things."

Gus didn't stop Mr. Ibrahim. I moved closer to Monsieur Duval and made sure Gus could see that I had a knife, too. And it was also coated in blood.

The smoke was getting thicker. "Help Kris," I cried to Monsieur Duval.

"Don't move," Gus said. His knife was pointed at Monsieur Duval's throat.

Monsieur Duval looked at me helplessly.

"The fire's spreading, Frankie. What are you going to do? Save her? Or save Monsieur Duval?" Gus asked sadistically. He was enjoying my torment.

I froze as I realized that I had no way to help either of them. If I left and saved myself, Kris and Monsieur Duval would both die. The spark of anger that had taken hold when I'd arrived on the stage flared to life again. I'd come too far to let Gus make me a victim again.

"Go, Frankie," Monsieur Duval said.

I looked at Kris, unconscious on the floor. I couldn't be responsible for her death, not after everything she'd done for me.

"No," I said. "I'm not leaving."

Gus laughed. "Fine, then you'll die like her," he said, nodding to Kris. "Like your family." He meant for his words to weaken me, but I wasn't going to fall for his tricks. He had a weakness, too.

I pulled the ankh out of my pocket. "You robbed Frances of her family and her future, and now you're going to lose her again."

For the first time since I'd arrived, Gus looked worried. In all the confusion, he'd forgotten about it. "Give that to me," he said.

"No. Let Monsieur Duval help Kris. Once they're safe, I'll give it to you." He didn't move. The knife was still aimed at Monsieur Duval. "If you don't, I throw the ankh into the fire. The metal will melt, and her soul will be gone forever."

Gus lowered his arm. He knew he was beat. Monsieur Duval darted over to Kris and untied the ropes. Kris's eyelids fluttered as Monsieur Duval hoisted her up onto his shoulder like a sack of flour.

"Give me the ankh," Gus said. He came toward me, his knife pointed at my chest.

I stood my ground. "No."

He lifted his knife higher. The blade glinted through the smoke. It was aimed at my throat. "I loved her."

"Funny way of showing it. Even now, you only care about yourself. You don't care what she wants. Her soul deserves freedom, not to be chained to you for eternity, in a body that she never wanted."

My body felt electrified as I waited for him to make the next move. I didn't have to wait long.

He grabbed for the ankh, but I held it out of his reach. He came at me again, wielding the knife. I spun away from him and found myself face-to-face with a wall of fire. The flames moved quickly, biting through the old, dry wood. I needed to get out of the warehouse. I side-stepped around Gus, trying to get closer to the fire exit.

"Give it to me!" he cried.

I'm sorry, Frances. I heaved the ankh as far as it would go into the fire. With a gut-wrenching howl, he charged into the flames and dropped to his knees, searching for it. The flames licked at him, but had no effect. His clothes didn't even catch fire.

The door to the fire escape was propped open. I could make a run for it and escape. And then what? Would he come after me again? Spend the next part of his eternity getting his revenge on me and everyone I cared about?

No, this needed to end, and I had the power to make it happen. "Gus!" I screamed.

"Ha!" He stood up, the ankh dangling from his fingers. The fire got louder. The floor below must have been engulfed by now. "I have her!"

He didn't see the knife fly through the air, but he felt it hit his thigh. Covered in Mr. Ibrahim's blood, the effect of the wound was instant. Gus gasped and fell to his knees. His knife clattered to the ground as his face contorted in monstrous anguish.

First his fingers, then his arms, and then the rest of him froze. Before my eyes, his face disintegrated and crumbled into ash. The ankh he'd held in his hand dropped to the floor.

For a moment, I stood staring at the pile of ashes in front of me, too shocked to move.

But then I had to move, because all around me, the walls were alive with flames. A spark landed on my hair. I batted it away. The room was engulfed now. The curtains around the stage fell to the ground. I crouched down and ran toward the fire escape. The smoke was too thick. Every breath was laboured. I wheezed, desperate for oxygen. The door was a little more than an arm's length away.

I felt myself slow down. It was an impossible distance. But I knew Kris had made it. So had Monsieur Duval and Mr. Ibrahim. They were safe.

The warehouse walls around me morphed into the outside of a house. It was on fire. I could feel its heat, but I wasn't in the flames. I was outside, watching. Someone was carrying me away from it, promising I'd be okay.

A crash jolted me back to my senses. Above me, a beam split and fell. I rolled out of the way, but fire leaped onto my clothes. I swatted at the flames, but they were spreading too fast.

I was being consumed.

32

I DIED AT THE WAREHOUSE.

At least, that was what I thought. I saw the bright white light and angels who flickered in and out. When I came to, I learned I wasn't in the afterlife, but a third-floor room located in the burn unit of St. Mary's Hospital. The angels were the nurses and doctors.

Kris's face was the first one I saw when my eyes fluttered open. I only managed a few minutes of wakefulness before I drifted back to sleep.

The next time I woke up, Kris was still there, but she wasn't alone.

Dr. Singh stood beside her. I only caught snippets of what he said. Kris filled me in later. He explained to both of us that burns like mine usually required skin grafts and multiple painful surgeries. But I didn't need any of that. "He said you're healing at an incredible rate and called you a medical miracle. What do you think of that?"

I had a feeding tube in my nose, and an IV in my arm. My whole body was bandaged. All I could do was blink to let her know, *I can hear you.*

Kris explained that it was all thanks to lamellar ichthyosis. The constant shedding of my condition meant that new skin was already growing under the burned tissue. The doctors had never seen anything like it and wanted to use me as a case study. Maybe my genetic abnormalities could be used to help other burn victims. For once, my alligator skin was a blessing, not a curse.

"Kris?" After not speaking for so long, saying anything out loud hurt. The IV tube was still stuck in my arm, pumping me full of antibiotics and nutrients, but I was awake for longer periods, which meant questions about what had happened came rushing back at me.

I couldn't live with blank spaces in my past anymore.

"What happened?" I asked in a rasping whisper.

Kris looked like she didn't know where to begin. "We can talk about this later. You should rest."

I shook my head. "Tell me."

She didn't look happy about it, but she started talking. "Monsieur Duval carried me out," Kris said. "An ambulance and fire truck had arrived by then. I came to once I got some oxygen. We tried to tell the firefighters you were still in there." Her voice caught and the rest of what she said came out haltingly. "They said it was too dangerous to send anyone back in." Kris wiped her eyes and blew her nose. "God, this is so hard," she said and took a deep breath. "I had to watch the building burn, knowing you were inside." She broke down in shoulder-shaking sobs.

I hated making her tell me, but I needed to know. If the firefighters hadn't gone in to get me, who had? "Monsieur Duval didn't listen. He raced past the barricade. They were all shouting at him to stop. He climbed back up the fire escape. He didn't come out right away, and I thought he was gone, too." I imagined Kris huddled under one of those gray flannel blankets, sitting in the back of an ambulance, smeared with soot and staring up at the fiery warehouse. "When he — when everyone saw him, it was like they froze in time. No one could believe it. And then, all of a sudden, they all came back to life, racing around to get you what you needed. He carried you down the fire escape. I don't know how he did it." But she did know. She'd been at the warehouse. Flames and smoke meant nothing to someone like Monsieur Duval.

"What about Mr. Ibrahim? And Fahid?" I asked.

"Fahid was arrested. He's actually been evading the police for a while on some internet fraud charges out east. Poor Mr. Ibrahim. He was shocked. He had no idea that his son was a wanted man. The performers didn't stick around, but Mr. Ibrahim did. He explained to the police that he and I were being held hostage by Gus and Fahid, and that you and Monsieur Duval had come to rescue us. He said that the fire had been set intentionally by Gus. And that Gus hadn't made it out of the building."

I opened my mouth to ask something else, but Kris shook her head and stood up. "No more questions. You need rest."

"But Monsieur Duval?" I persisted. "What happened to him?"

She shrugged. "I don't know. After he saved you, he disappeared."

"Do you think he's gone? Like really gone? He knows how to end his life now."

Kris got quiet. "I don't know, Frankie." She turned off the light. "I'm serious — no more questions. I'll be back tomorrow. Sleep well."

After she left, I lay in my bed thinking about Monsieur Duval. He had a way out of his immortality now. Would he take it?

I gained strength daily. A week later, I could stay awake for hours at a time, and my pain medication had been decreased. There was talk about starting physiotherapy soon. Confident that I was going to survive, Kris had gone back to work part-time, mornings only. The case she'd been working on wasn't yet resolved, but the people behind it were in custody. Dealing with the kids involved took a toll on her. I wished she had an easier job, but I knew that if she wasn't there to help, those kids might have no one.

"Knock, knock," she said from the doorway. "You awake?"

I pushed myself up to a sitting position. I still had bandages covering most of my body, but moving around was getting easier.

"I am now," I said.

Kris dumped her jacket and work bag onto the chair beside my bed. Sunlight streamed into the room. I didn't mind it as much as I'd used to. A brush with death did that to you.

As soon as I saw Kris's face, I knew something was up. "I've been doing some digging," she said. "I think I found out something about your past."

"What?" I asked.

She reached into her bag and pulled out a file folder. My heart sank. Not another File. "I did a search for house fires up to six weeks prior to you being found in the alley. There were hundreds of hits, but only a few had multiple fatalities. I looked at all of them, and then I found this." She opened the folder and showed me the article. *House Fire Kills Family of Five.*

As soon as I saw the byline location, vomit rose in my throat. I knew this place. I pushed the file away. "I can't look at it," I said. What if it said the fire had been my fault? Even if it had been an accident. How would I survive knowing that? I'd rather live with a blank space than that kind of guilt.

Kris shook her head and pushed it back at me. "You need to know. This part of your past isn't going away."

I shut my eyes. The echoing frantic screams. The heat pulsing off the flames. "Frankie," Kris said gently. "You're ready."

She started to read. "'A tragic fire in Allenby has claimed the lives of five members of a local family. The Allenby Volunteer Fire Department was called to a farm just after 2:00 a.m. on Friday. When they arrived, the home was already fully engulfed in flames. Investigators believe the fire was caused by a *malfunctioning dryer* in the basement.'" She paused and glanced at me. "'Some of the remains are too badly burned to be identified, but all five members of the family were home at the time of the fire.'" Kris met my eyes.

I let out a breath I didn't realize I'd been holding. "It wasn't me."

Kris shook her head. "You couldn't have done that on purpose. You wouldn't have known how."

"Gus might've."

"Maybe. Or maybe it was an accident, and Gus was there at just the right time. There's a photo of your family. Do you want to see it?" she asked.

"I don't know."

Kris didn't push it. "I'll leave the photo in the file. It's here when you want it," she said and opened the drawer in the bedside table to tuck it away.

"Do they look like me?" I asked.

Kris paused. "You mean your skin?"

I nodded.

"No."

I held out my hand for the photo. "Okay, show me."

It was one of those family photos that you could get at Walmart. The parents stood behind three children. Everyone was wearing jeans and white shirts. The older sister's hands rested gently on her brother's shoulders. I was in the photo, too, grinning, my teeth glaringly white. My hair had been braided, and two elastics with daisies were fastened to the ends. But it was my skin that I couldn't stop staring at. It glowed an unnatural tan colour, the edges too sharp. My scaly skin had been erased, Photoshopped. The five of us sat in the posed photo, caught forever in time.

They looked so normal. *We* looked so normal. My mother had a short, sensible haircut. She looked sort of mousy with her wire-rimmed glasses. My older sister had braces, and her hair hung past her shoulders. My brother had a scar on his chin; it hadn't been erased. Had I asked for my skin to be changed? Or had my parents done it so that I'd look like them?

"Your parents were Matt and Holly. Your sister was named Janna, and Mark was your brother. You were Grace."

"Grace," I said out loud, trying to connect the name with the person in the picture. "Do I look like a Grace?" The name meant nothing to me. There was no echo of it in my head. No fireworks went off when I heard it.

"You're Frankie to me."

I was about to give her back the photo, then changed my mind. "Can I keep it?" I asked.

"Of course. It's yours."

On the table beside my bed was a water glass, my art supplies, and a cactus that Kris had brought. She'd thought it was more my style than flowers. I propped the photo up against the clay pot. *Janna, Mark, and Grace,* I repeated in my head. *And my parents, Holly and Matt.*

I thought the memories were buried too deep to resurface, but as I drifted to sleep that night, they appeared. Blurry at first, and then in sharper focus, my family from when I was a child floated out of my subconscious: the five of us on Christmas morning; a picnic in the summer; jumping on a trampoline; my mother tucking me into bed and kissing me on the forehead. "Good night, Grace," she'd whispered, brushing her lips against my scaly-skinned forehead. "I love you."

"Love you, too," I'd said and burrowed deeper into the blankets, warm, safe, and loved.

33

WHEN KRIS CAME TO SEE ME AFTER WORK the next day, she had good news. "Nurse Arlene says you're ready for visitors."

I snorted. "I'm sure there's a long lineup."

"Actually, there is," Jessica said as she walked in with her grandfather.

"Frankie's sarcasm is still intact," Kris assured them.

"I can't believe you're here!" I blurted. I had no makeup on because I wasn't allowed, but part of me had also stopped caring. Being in a burn unit had shown me there were people a lot worse off than me. I waited for a flash of revulsion from Jessica or Mr. Ibrahim, but none came. They were too concerned about what I'd been through to care about my skin.

Mr. Ibrahim passed me a gift bag, and I noticed the cut on his hand had healed. Only a small pink line was left as a reminder of what had happened in the warehouse.

"We won't stay long," he said. "We were so worried about you." He motioned to the gift. "Open it."

I pulled a box out of the bag and lifted the lid. An eye stared back at me. Well, not a real eye — a stylized Egyptian eye. It was a large brass medallion that I recognized from his stall. "The Eye of Horus," Mr. Ibrahim said. "A protector. It will look over you when we can't."

I looked at him, startled. "We?"

"He told me everything," Jessica said. "He had to. Hussein's blood is in me, as well."

Mr. Ibrahim nodded thoughtfully. "You were destined to be friends." The idea had occurred to me, too. It was because of Jessica that I'd met Mr. Ibrahim and learned about the ankh and the curse. What would have happened if I hadn't followed her into the washroom that day to give her back her sketchbook? Or if she'd pushed me away when I offered to help?

Jessica cleared her throat and with a dramatic gesture, pulled a card out of her purse. "And this is from Mr. Kurtis."

Dear Frankie,

Art class isn't the same without you. I made a reference to the Cure, and no one got it.

One of the reasons I love teaching art is that sometimes I get to see a side of students no one else can. It's not about the talent of a student, but their willingness to open up and share who they really are. You have the unique ability to be both talented and honest in your art. Never change that about yourself.

Especially when you become a famous graphic novelist — because that's going to happen! I told a friend who works at a publishing company in the city how talented you are and about your work. They want to see the whole thing. When you're up for it, give me a call and we'll talk.

Sincerely,
Mr. Kurtis

I couldn't stop a smile from spreading across my face. I passed the card to Kris so she could read it out loud. "Oh, Frankie, congratulations!"

"It hasn't been accepted yet," I said, but I was blushing with pride.

"*Yet*," Jessica said.

We chatted for a while longer. Mr. Ibrahim told me that without Fahid to work at the flea market, Jessica had been coming in a few days after school and on the weekends. "She's a quick study," Mr. Ibrahim said. His eyes sparkled.

Jessica showed me the new Instagram page she'd set up for the booth. Each photo was artfully arranged to showcase one of the artifacts. "This one got over a thousand likes," she said.

"Business is picking up," Mr. Ibrahim said. "I don't know how from a few pictures, but ..."

"You have to change with the times, Grandpa."

"Bah! Change is overrated," he said. When it was time for them to leave, I asked Mr. Ibrahim if he could stay for a minute.

"Have you seen him?" I asked quickly.

"Philippe? No. Not since the fire."

I nodded. I'd expected as much. "If you do, will you tell him I'd like to see him?"

Mr. Ibrahim smiled. "Of course."

After they left, I pulled out my sketchbook. My hands were stiff. The pencil lines looked clumsy compared to what I'd used to be able to do, but I had to start somewhere. I knew how I wanted Frances's story to end. The pictures I drew showed Frances leaving on the train. Gus ran after her, but she didn't try to jump. She knew her future lay ahead, not behind. In my sketchbook at least, Frances found freedom.

34

WHEN KRIS ARRIVED A FEW DAYS LATER, she had some papers in her hand. "I've got news," she said sitting in the chair beside my bed.

"Good or bad?"

Instead of telling me, she dropped the papers on my lap. "You tell me."

"What are they?" They were official looking and already filled in. "Order of Adoption" was written across the top. In the box marked "applicant" it read *Kristina Steffanson* and then my name. *Frances Doe.*

"Are you serious?" I asked, looking at her. She nodded. Her eyes were shining, the same way they had before Comicon. It had been a long time since I'd seen her look so excited. But the hesitation, the wariness that kept everyone at arm's length, stopped me from smiling back. "I'm seventeen. What's the point? I'll be an adult soon. Your responsibility —"

Kris cut me off. "I want to be your mom, Frankie. And I want you to be my daughter."

"But —"

She shook her head. "There're no buts. This is what I want. I applied months ago, but then the fire and that case I was working on slowed things down. The judge gave her final approval today." She pointed to the signature on the back page.

"So it's legal. Just like that? I'm not Frankie Doe anymore."

Kris gave me a long, meaningful look. She reached over and took my hand. It wasn't bandaged anymore. "That's all behind you. You're Frankie Steffanson now."

Hearing her say my name brought tears to my eyes.

"What do you think?" she asked.

Deep down, it was what I had always wanted but had been too afraid to hope for. Everything I'd been through, all the stuff before the fire, had taught me what Frances had learned, too — the world wasn't kind to people like us.

But sometimes, there was a ray of light. There was a Kris, or a Mathilde.

I was afraid to nod. What if it was a dream and if I nodded, I'd wake up?

"Frankie?" Kris asked again.

I looked at her: the woman who knew all my flaws and loved me, not in spite of them, but because of them. "Frankie Steffanson," I repeated quietly. "It sounds good, doesn't it?"

Kris nodded. "That's how I've always thought of you."

I didn't need to hide from my past anymore. I knew who I was and now, because of Kris, I had a future.

Jessica came to see me a few days later. I'd texted her the news about my adoption and that Frankie Doe was no more. I'd been reborn as Frankie Steffanson, and she'd been almost as excited about it as I was.

Her hair was curled today, and she was dressed up a little, the way she used to look. I wondered if she'd found other friends to hang out with at school. I silenced that voice. She was here and that was what mattered. Plus, we had a bond that ran deep. Our secrets were going to keep us connected. I let her get settled into the chair by my bed.

"I didn't want to ask while your grandpa was here —"

"About Tyler Jefferies?" she guessed.

I nodded.

"The Monday after the fire, I begged my parents to let me stay home. I was a mess after hearing what happened to you and Grandpa, and the stuff on social media had gotten worse over the weekend. Of course, they said no." She frowned at the memory. "I didn't think I could face the Aprils without you?"

I gave a wry grin at her use of the word *Aprils*.

"I was going to try to do what we'd done, hide in the washroom until first period and then sneak into class. But as soon as I walked into the school, I regretted it. All over the walls were photocopied pictures of me with the word *LIAR* over them. I just froze, right in the middle of the entrance. I couldn't believe what I was seeing. A bunch of the girls were standing together against one wall, laughing like it was the funniest thing they'd ever seen. Of course, Sadie was there, the ringleader. I'd already quit the volleyball team. You'd think that would be enough, but no. She wanted to break me.

"I didn't know what to do. Ignore them? Go into the washroom and hide? Or just leave? I wanted to leave. Transfer schools, even. The thought of facing them every day was too much. And without you ..." She shook her head. "I felt helpless. Like I had no one to turn to. I just wanted to give up."

I remembered that feeling so clearly. Hearing Jessica talk about it brought the pain back to me.

"But I thought about you lying in the hospital and how pissed off you'd be if I did. I think I was more scared of your reaction than of dealing with the Aprils!" Jessica smirked at me. "I had a WWFD moment — What Would Frankie Do," she clarified. "I knew if you'd been there, you would have told me to take the posters down. So that's what I did. I went up and down the halls, ripping them down. I could hear the girls laughing at me like it was all a joke. That's when I started getting mad. If one of them had been assaulted, I would've tried to help, not turned on them." Jessica's face turned fiery. "Their reaction violated me as much as Tyler had. I'd never trusted him, but I did trust them. I thought they were my friends." She shook her head in disgust. "I decided I was done being the victim. So I saved a poster and brought it to Ms. Hughes, our volleyball coach."

"What did she do?"

Jessica got quiet. "She asked why they'd put them up. By this point, there was no reason to lie. I ended up telling her everything. About what Tyler did and what happened when I told Sadie. I told her why I'd quit the team. Ms. Hughes was super pissed. She stormed out of her office and dragged Sadie to the principal's office. I don't know what happened in there, but Sadie got suspended from school for the rest of the week and from the team for three games. When she came back, she gave me a handwritten letter of apology. And Ms. Hughes offered to take me to a counsellor or a doctor, whoever I want to talk to. I've gone a few times. It's been good."

I gave her an encouraging smile before asking, "And Tyler?"

Jessica bit her lip. "The police know. A cop came to school to get my statement. It turns out there's this other girl —"

"Oh my god," I said. My heart lurched for her. Jessica nodded.

"She goes to another school, but she's come forward." Jessica's voice trailed off. "There might be others, too."

I reached out to hold her hand. Mine was scaly in some spots, and new pink skin grew in others. Jessica didn't hesitate before grabbing it.

I knew how hard it was to open up about some things. It was like Kris always said, you had to clean the wound before it could heal. I had scars all over my body, but it was the injuries no one could see that were the most painful. Jessica had bared herself to me. It was only fair that I did the same.

"I need to tell you something," I paused, balling up the bed sheets into my fist. "When I was twelve, I moved in with my second foster mom. Things were fine at first, I mean, not great, but I was getting by. Then she started dating this guy ..." I looked at Jessica. "He seemed super nice at first. She really loved him and kept saying how happy she was. But it was all an act. The only reason the guy was interested in her was because of me. He took pictures of me. Because of my skin. Then, he sold them to the highest bidder."

Jessica shuddered. "Oh my god. That's horrible."

This won't hurt, he'd promised as he held up the camera and snapped the first photo. But it had hurt. He'd exploited me. I'd been powerless against his roving eyes and the click of his camera. "I thought it was my fault. He said if I told anyone, my foster mom would go to jail."

"What happened?"

"I told Kris, finally. It was going to go to trial, but he pleaded guilty. He got five years." Five years for him and a lifetime for me. "His name is Aaron Mosley. I don't like to say it out loud, but I should. Everyone should know who he is and what he did."

"They should tattoo it on his forehead. We have to live with what they did, why don't they?" Jessica's eyes flashed with anger.

I wished I had an answer for her.

35

IT HAD BEEN THREE MONTHS SINCE THE FIRE. I could walk on my own now, and the feeding tube had been removed. The doctors had met and decided it was time for me to go home. I'd still have weekly physiotherapy appointments, but I'd hit all the benchmarks. There was no reason to keep me in the hospital.

It felt like leaving a cocoon. I'd been safe and protected here. Once I got outside, I'd have to fend for myself again.

There was a knock on the door. I wasn't expecting anyone. Kris was at work until dinner time. "Come in," I called.

Monsieur Duval stepped into the room. I gaped at him, at a loss for words.

He was in a suit today. A white shirt unbuttoned at the neck, no tie. He looked like a handsome businessman. "Sorry to intrude," he said.

I still wasn't allowed to wear makeup. And I wasn't sure I wanted to anymore. Monsieur Duval's eyes turned tender as he looked at me. "Such a marvel," he whispered.

"I'm glad to see you. I thought maybe you'd —" I broke off trying to think of the right word. "Ended things," I said finally.

He gave a knowing smile. "I thought about it. Time does stretch ahead of us." He glanced at the chair beside my bed. "May I sit?"

I nodded and watched as he moved gracefully, smoothing out the crease in his pants as he crossed his legs.

"I have something to tell you," I said. The words I needed to say stalled on my tongue. I'd thought about them a lot and didn't know if I'd get the chance to tell him. But here he was.

I'd named Aaron Mosley and his crimes against me. I couldn't let Monsieur Duval off the hook for what he'd done. It might have been a hundred years ago, but it was still wrong. "It's about Frances." A flicker of sadness crossed his face. Still, after all these years, he missed her. "In my dreams, she didn't want to be onstage. She hated it."

Monsieur Duval gave me a long look and frowned. "There are many things I regret in this life, Frankie, but what I put Frances through is the biggest. I thought everyone would see her for *who* she was, but instead, they saw her for *what* she was."

"The world is not kind to us."

He sighed like the weight of the world rested on his shoulders. "I called myself her papa, but I should have protected her, like Mathilde wanted to do. She deserved a better life than the one I gave her."

I hoped Frances, wherever she was, knew this and forgave him.

Hearing the pain in his voice made what I had to say next even harder. "There's something else. It's about the ankh," I started. "I destroyed it in the fire."

Monsieur Duval sat back in the chair and watched me, surprisingly unconcerned. "It was a bit of sentimentality on my part, imagining you with the ankh." He reached under his shirt and lifted out a chain with an identical ankh to the one lost in the fire. "But I could never have given her away. Frances has been with me all this time."

I stared at the one in his hands. Of course, that made sense. Why would he have ever let her go? "But I thought it was because of the ankh that I was receiving her memories," I said, confused.

"Perhaps Frances realized what danger you were in and found a way to communicate with you. Souls can be powerful when they want to be. I don't like to think of Frances as trapped in here. It's not a prison. It's her home. She can come and go as she pleases." When he placed it back against his chest, I saw how close it lay to his heart. Monsieur Duval leaned forward in his chair. "I came to say goodbye, Frankie. The troupe and I are leaving tonight."

"To go where?"

"Yuri has always wanted to go back to Russia, so that's our plan. He bought a beautiful estate just after the war, an eighteenth-century manor house. We plan to while away a few years there. I'm considering writing a book."

"About?"

"A brave young woman who faces her demons more than once."

My throat tightened. "How will it end?"

He smiled. "Happily, I think. It's what she deserves." He got up to go, but before he got to the door, I called to him.

"Monsieur Duval?"

He looked at me. I held his gaze for a moment as memories of the circus washed over me. "She knew you loved her."

"Thank you, Frankie," he said and bowed his head to me. "That means more than you know."

After he'd gone, the silence of the room sank into me. All the loose ends were tied up, from the past and the present. I had people in my life who cared about me. And my skin — well, in an unexpected way, my skin had saved my life. I was healing.

I sighed contentedly. The Eye of Horus, my gift from Mr. Ibrahim, gazed at me from the opposite wall. "Maybe I won't need your protection after all," I whispered.

From my bed, I could have sworn that it winked at me.

Acknowledgements

I'D LIKE TO THANK THE TEAM AT DUNDURN, specifically Kathryn Lane, Jenny McWha, Melissa Kawaguchi, Sophie Paas-Lang, Stephanie Ellis, Kendra Martin, Lisa Marie Smith, and Elham Ali. Thank you to Catharine Chen for the copy edits.

Cindy Kochanski read the book when it was a bit of a dumpster fire ... okay, possibly more than a bit. As usual, she tactfully suggested some edits which led to rewrites and stopped me from throwing the whole thing into an actual fire. Rebecca Wesselius was also an early reader and it was thanks to her encouragement that I kept working on it. A huge thank you to Jess Shulman, who is a great editor and pointed me in the right direction with subtle and humorous comments. She made revisions enjoyable. Thank you to Jamie Gatta, who did illustrations for many of the characters. Seeing them on paper breathed life into Frankie's art.

On a personal note, a lot of this book was revised during the #MeToo era. I'd like to acknowledge the strength that it takes for anyone to come forward to share their story. I've invented Frankie's, but sadly, Jessica's is based on someone close to me. I hope the lasting impact of #MeToo will be that the shame that once fell on the victim will land where it should: on the perpetrator.

About the Author

COLLEEN NELSON is a teacher and author from Winnipeg, Manitoba. Her previous YA books include White Pine nominee and Schwartz Award winner *Sadia*, as well as *Spin*, *Blood Brothers*, and *Finding Hope*. She has also written the middle grade books *Harvey Comes Home* and *Harvey Holds His Own*. As an avid middle grade and YA reader, Colleen is involved in a number of literacy initiatives, such as the Manitoba Young Readers Choice Award, MG Lit Online Book Club, and the Canadian Children's Book Centre. Over the years, Colleen has lived in New York and Japan, but the pull of the prairies brought her back to Winnipeg. When not writing or teaching, Colleen likes to run, read, and travel. A few other things Colleen likes: chocolate, winning at Scrabble, tulips, and watching her dog, Rosie, chase squirrels.